A

Wager
for a
Bride

By Amy Horikami

Dedication

This is to you Gerret! None of this would be possible without your constant support and love.

To my little sister, Anne!
I love going over ideas with you, and I hope this book has enough pride and prejudice vibes to make you love Ronin just as much as you love Darcy!

No part of this book may be reproduced in any form whatsoever, whether by graphic, visual, electronic, film, microfilm, tape recording, or any other means, without prior permission of the author.

This work is a work of fiction. The characters, names, incidents, places, and dialogues are products of the author's imagination and are not to be construed as real and are used fictitiously. They are in no way shape or form related to any real persons, places, things, and are coincidental if such a case occurs.

Copyright © 2022 Amy Horikami

All rights reserved

Chapter 1

RONIN

I signaled to my men to stay low and just observe the scene before us. We were here since the ogre raids have been occurring more frequently in our kingdom. That was not what worried me though. What concerned me was that they were becoming more calculated and had some formation to them and I wanted to know why.

These incompetent beasts were not smart enough to organize a raid with such precision and stealth that they were recently undertaking, so I knew someone else must be the intellect behind it. I looked to Caden, my captain, who was hidden with his group of men among the trees on the north side of the forest. I signaled to him to stay low and observe. Our superior vision made it easy to communicate in these vast woods. He nodded, telling me he understood and signaled to his men to do the same.

I stalked forward and crouched low behind the tall grass to get closer to the ugly brutes, who were all muscle and no brains. Ogres were large beasts with ivory tusks that jutted out of their bottom jaw. Their skin was the color of decayed swamp and their smell about matched that description too.

That was when I noticed dark cloaks that blended against the rocky mountain cave before me, and I immediately knew who was behind it. The dark fae. Then, a tall man with pointed ears, just like ours, walked out with the leader of the Ogres, Dret, and it all made sense. It was the Dark Fae Prince, Devron was his name if I recall correctly, who must be the mastermind behind these raids.

His dark hair matched his appearance and the power he held. I would be a fool if I didn't recognize a formidable foe when I met one. He was uncanny and one of the most powerful fae I have ever encountered. Luckily, our meetings were few and far between, and today we were just here to observe. He could take out a village if he so desired with the power he held. He was also the cousin to his majesty, King Leon of Llor of the Light Fae Lands, which created a bigger problem since we knew the dark prince's brother, King Kadrell of the Dark Fae Lands of Bethrel, wanted to conquer and rule our kingdom. His ambition was strong, but our army was ten times larger than his, so his threats were harmless…until now.

If his brother was working with the ogres and who knows what other dreadful creatures that hid in these mountains, we could have our work cut out for us.

I signaled to my men and Caden to fall back. I had the information I needed. Now that I knew the whole story, it was time to form our strategy on how to deal with these brutes.

A couple of hours later, we could finally see the great stone castle ahead of us. Its beauty was a timeless piece of work with countless spires and intricate designs that only the fae could accomplish. It was what we called home. We rode quickly, needing to get the information to our king as soon as possible before another raid happened upon our kingdom. The villages that lay on the outskirts of our land were already suffering from their destruction.

"How soon do you think they'll attack?" my captain asked from his steed galloping next to mine.

"I'm not sure. I hope the scouts I left there to observe for the next few days will gather all the intellect we need to form a more solid plan. We have enough now to inform our king and start making preparations."

"With the dark prince behind it, we might have to adjust our strategy."

He was right. The ogres were easy to handle with the number of men I had, but the power the dark fae brought to their forces would make it more difficult. I trusted my men, and adding more strategy and magic to our routine would not be difficult.

"You are right, but adjusting our training will not be difficult. You men have never failed me before. Give me a few days and I'll have our new regimen ready."

"Yes, Commander."

We finally made it back to the castle and headed towards the stables. I hopped down from the saddle and patted the large dappled gray stallion on the neck, who nudged my chest with his nose and then searched my hand for a treat.

"Easy there, Altivo." I chuckled at the horse, eagerly searching my body for an apple or a carrot I sometimes gave him. "You'll get your deserved oats soon." He shook his mane as if to tell me that wasn't good enough. I grabbed his reins and led him to the stableboy, who was waiting for me to hand my horse off to him.

"Here you go Tristan, make sure he gets a good rub down and extra oats. He deserves it."

"Yes, commander." The eager young fae nodded to me as he took the reins from my hand. His father worked in the stables, but I knew the boy wanted to be a soldier. He would often watch my men and me sparring. One time I caught him in the training yard by himself with one of our training swords he took from the armory. Instead of scolding him, I taught him a few moves in negotiation that he would not take from the armory again. He has been good on his word so far.

"Maybe later, if your father allows it, I'll show you some extra moves with the sword. How does that sound?"

His freckled face glowed as his smile stretched from pointed ear to pointed ear.

"Really! Oh, boy! I can't wait!" He threw his fist in the air, then looked at me with shock and nodded his head, trying to act dignified. "I meant, thanks, commander."

I ruffled the young fae's short brown hair and his grin returned, making me laugh out loud.

"Good! I'm looking forward to it."

Then turning on my heel, I made my way into the castle.

Chapter 2

RONIN

I went down the large white-marbled halls towards the center of the castle and stopped in front of the large door with our kingdom's crest proudly displayed on the dark wood. Two swords crossed each other with a crown and white rose in the middle, its thorns wrapping around each of the swords. It was the King's study where my closest friend usually spent most of his days. We were like brothers, his majesty and I. My father was commander to the former king, and I took over once he retired. He trained us from when we were young fae, and we have been close ever since.

Which is why I threw open the door instead of knocking to announce my presence.

"Ronin! Don't you ever knock!" his majesty turned to me from where he was standing with an exasperated look. He was tall like me, the only mutual thing we had in our appearances besides the short style we kept our hair. My build was thick with muscle, while his was lean, but not any less fierce than most of my men. He could keep his own. I would know; growing up sparring proved it time and time again. My dark brown hair was a deep contrast to his shocking blonde, which was nearly white.

"Oh, Leon, and give up on the element of surprise? You know me better than that. Plus, I must use my title as an advantage sometimes."

"I don't think *commander* allows for such intrusions. Even my advisors knock."

"Are you sure?"

He rolled his eyes and huffed out a chuckle.

I made my way over to him and we slapped each other on the back and smiled in greeting. I noticed maps displayed before him on a large table with some navigating tools.

"I have some news for you."

"Please tell me it's better than what I have been dealing with."

"It's about the ogres."

He turned, giving me his full attention as I relayed the information about his cousin being involved with the raids and assisting the ogres.

He leaned against the table with his head hanging low and rubbed his eyes with one hand.

"Are you sure it was him?" he looked up, and I could tell the weight of the kingdom was heavy on his shoulders.

"I'm positive. I would know your cousin anywhere."

"Why all of this now." He turned and leaned over the maps placing his hands on the table before him.

"I have this alliance I need to fulfill." He motioned towards the stack of parchment.

"Alliance?"

"With Retna."

"Has five years passed already?"

"Yes, and I don't have time to take a bride when I have all this going on."

"Maybe we can delay the alliance for another year or so. At least until the raids have stopped."

Our kingdom had an old alliance with the little town of Retna, which was right outside our eastern borders. Every five years, one of our fae was chosen to take a maiden from their town as a bride for themselves. In return, we protected the little town from ogres and other foul creatures that dwelled in our forests. It was easy to protect the little town since our kingdom resided between them and the dreadful creatures.

"No, we can't delay it. It keeps the peace between us."

"Maybe we can find someone else to take your place? I can talk to my men and…"

He turned to me with wide eyes and a sly smile on his face.

"No, Your Majesty."

"Please, Ronin. It would be perfect! You with a young maiden on your arm." He put his hand over his heart and mockingly sighed.

"No."

"You know, I could order you, and you would…"

"Don't." I cut him off. Best friend or not, he knew I would not put up with his overbearing requests. I quickly thought of an excuse to leave and remembered a young fae I promised to practice sparring with soon.

"Find someone else. I need to leave. I have an eager young fae waiting for me in the training grounds with which I promised to spar."

"Hmmm..." The king tapped his chin, then jumped up from leaning on his table and wrapped one arm around my shoulder.

"How about a little wager then, old friend? You and *me* in a friendly match."

"You? Sparring? You haven't beaten me since we were young fae." I scoffed and shoved his arms off my shoulder.

"So, what are you worried about? It will be just like old times." he taunted, opening his arms wide in a challenge.

"Nothing. I don't have time for this *or* a wife."

"Come on, Ronin." He begged. "If I lose, I'll go get me a bride, and you never have to be chosen to fulfill the alliance… ever. But, if I win…"

"No." I turned and left his study only to have him follow me.

"Why not? You are lonely. Don't you want someone to go home to? A family?"

"My men *are* my family. I'm trying to keep *your* kingdom safe from all these ogre raids. I do not have time to worry about some girl who does not know how to care for herself. I have more important things to worry about."

We finally made it out to the training yard, and Tristan was sitting on the fence waiting for me. He hopped down and started to make his way over to us.

"Your Majesty." The young fae bowed to Leon, turned to me, and asked, "what's wrong?"

I turned to Leon and gave him a look to keep his mouth shut about our conversation, but he already had a mischievous grin on his face as he turned toward Tristan.

"Oh, your commander doesn't think he can beat me in a little sparring contest."

"The commander? Of course, he can...uh...I...meant..."

Leon laughed. "Such confidence this young fae has in you. You wouldn't want to let him down now, would you?"

"No, it's that I don't gamble my freedom away, Your Majesty. Something that Tristan should learn as well."

"It is not a gamble, just a friendly wager. You don't even have to marry the girl, just bring her back here." Then he looked at me with all seriousness. "Please, Ronin, I need this."

I let out an exasperated groan, letting him know how I felt about the whole situation.

"Fine! Let us get this over with. I have more important things to do."

Leon smirked. "As do I."

We quickly changed into our training leathers and met back at the training yard. I hopped the fence to greet my friend, who was eagerly waiting for me with a sword in his hand as I looked around at our vast audience. No doubt that the stableboy spread the word while we changed. Tristan was straddling the fence, eager to watch our bout. I nodded to him and turned to Leon, who was twisting his sword around in a taunting manner.

"Well, Your Majesty. I would hate to see you lose in front of all your *loyal* subjects. I'll give you a chance to back out and save yourself the embarrassment." A few chuckles came from the crowd, and I was hoping he would take the bait. He was no match for me. My men rarely bested me as it was, and we trained daily.

"Oh, Ronin, such words for a man, who is about to eat them."

Nobody was shocked by our taunting. They knew we were close and had high respect for one another despite our jabs.

Leon lifted his sword and arms towards my men as he sauntered around the field. A roar of cheers went up for their King, and I rolled my eyes at his theatrics.

"Enough, Your Majesty, let's begin!"

I stepped forward to start our wager. Bringing our swords up, we danced around each other when the king finally made the first move. I blocked his strike, twisting my sword away from him. Then, I brought my weapon back around to have him block my attack. We went back and forth for about ten minutes, and I could tell he was growing tired. His stamina was not as strong as mine since he spent most of his days dealing with politics now that he was king. This wager would be over soon, and I could go about my day with more important matters that needed attending to. He would just have to fulfill his duty to Retna instead of pawning it off on me.

I brought my arm up to give the final blow that would corner him and bring a stop to our fighting.

"Aaaaahhh" A young scream came from the high wall, and I turned to see Tristan falling from the post where he was watching our duel. One of my men caught him, to my relief, and I quickly turned back to finish what we started only to find a sword at my throat and Leon with a wicked grin on his lips.

"Distracted Commander? Isn't that the first rule you teach? Don't ever let your guard down."

I growled and dropped my sword on the dirt, signaling my surrender.

Then he chuckled, "A deal is a deal."

I berated myself for letting the distraction make me lose the wager. I had no words; I rarely lost a fight. I couldn't be mad at the stableboy for losing his balance, it was my own fault for being caught off guard.

"Well, it seems my work here is finished." He smirked and offered me a low bow, then turned and left the training grounds with an overconfident gait.

"Come to my study later, Ronin," he called out to me, "we'll go over the details for getting your *bride-to*-be. Because you, my friend, are getting married!"

My men chuckled at the king's retort and my demise. I turned to glare at them, my pride getting the better of me. Most of them stopped, but their eyes were shining with humor as they watched us.

I took a deep breath and ordered my men to get back to training.

"I'm sorry, commander." Came a small voice behind me.

I turned and saw the ten-year-old with his head hung low and cheeks red with shame. It wasn't his fault I lost the wager, and I hated seeing him feel bad for my error. I put a hand on his shoulder, and he looked up at me with a frown.

"I didn't mean to make you lose. I slipped on the fence, and I…"

"It's okay. It wasn't your fault. While our King already told you the first rule, the second is to move on from your mistakes, and that mistake over there," I nodded toward the training area, "was solely mine."

A grin spread across his face, and I ruffled his hair again.

"Now, I think I promised you a lesson."

"Oh, boy! After what I just saw, I am ready! I am going to be just like you, commander!"

It was my turn to chuckle. At least *his* spirit wasn't broken. For me, I was about to get an unwanted bride.

Chapter 3

3 Weeks Later

LILLIAN

"Oh, this intricate pattern is absolutely beautiful, Lillian." Madam Olgath, the seamstress I worked for, was holding up the gown I was currently working on. I decided to add some lace to the cuffs and hem of the dress to match the ivory material.

"Thank you," I told the tall, thin woman who pretty much dressed the entire town of Retna.

"I knew I saw talent when you came to me those two years ago. Now, look at you creating these stunning designs on your own. Anyone who wears one of these will be the talk of the festival and will surely be picked as the next fae bride."

"Oh, I don't know about that." I flushed at her compliment and pushed the needle back into the cloth to finish another stitch.

"Do not doubt yourself, deary. When the gown is finished, let me know. I have a spot in the shop window that will display it perfectly and undoubtedly draw in customers.

I nodded to her and continued the small stitches along the hem of the gown. I found peace in this little shop, which was so different from my own home.

The bell above the door rang, indicating we had a customer in our shop. I heard Madam Olgath heading to the front, so I stayed put to finish my work. She was better with customers anyway. I was the town drunk's daughter, and most people treated me indifferently, except for my two closest friends.

"Lillian!" I would know that voice anywhere, and looked up to see my auburn-haired friend, Claira, followed by Helen, the dark-haired beauty of our group and Claira's cousin. I put my work down and greeted them each with warm hugs. They were such a light in my life, and our little trio was so close.

"The festival is tomorrow, and I can't wait to see who the next bride will be." Claira swooned as she browsed the workroom full of material.

"I hear the fae are stunning, and their ears are pointed at the end," Helen added. They both turned to me.

"What about you, Lillian? Are you excited to go to the festival?"

"Oh, I don't know. It is not like they will pick any of us. Our birthdays are still a couple of months away." We all were seventeen still. The maiden chosen to be the next fae bride was always of age.

"Yes, but that doesn't mean we can't look or dance with them." Claira started to twirl around the workroom as if she had a partner in her arms.

"Oh, Claira, you're such a romantic." Helen sighed, and I let out a small giggle at her theatrics. She made everything so much fun when we were together.

"Speaking of the festival, guess what I barely finished this morning?" I looked at Helen while getting up from my seat and headed towards the back to where the finished gowns were located, and I returned with a large box.

"Is it?" she looked at me eagerly, then at the box in my hands.

"Oh, do open it, Helen! Let us have a look!" Claira declared anxiously. I smiled at my friend's eagerness and handed Helen the box. She untied the ribbon and took off the lid eagerly as we watched her, anticipating her reaction. She pulled out a beautiful purple gown, and held it against her body, swishing the skirt back and forth, ending in a spin.

"Oh, Lillian! It is beautiful." She set it on the seat and came over to hug me. "You always do such lovely work."

"I'm so glad you like it." I spent extra care and time to get all the cuts right. It would fit her to perfection. I even added some ruffles that were currently in style.

"You better watch out, Helen; you might be the one chosen with this gown on." Claira teased.

We talked about our plans for the festival while I continued to stitch the lace on the ivory gown. I was grateful Madam Olgath let them visit me as long as I didn't let them get between me and my work. I never did, and they never stayed long.

"We should start early and head to the bakery for some treats while they are hot and fresh." Claira said, then looked at me, "Are you working tomorrow, Lillian? Surely, Madam Olgath will let you enjoy the festival."

"No, she said I could have it off and enjoy the festivities."

"Oh, good!" They both exclaimed in unison as they clapped their hands at the joyful news.

After a short while, we finally said our goodbyes, and I finished my work while helping a few more customers. Many women came in to pick up their gowns for the upcoming festival. Luckily, only a few needed minor adjustments.

The day went by faster than usual. The evening was here before I knew it, and it was time to close the shop for the day. My anxiety started to rise as I was putting the pins away. My shakiness made me drop the container that held them, and they burst across the floor. I quickly bent to pick them up, hoping the seamstress wouldn't see my blunder. Suddenly, a shadow was in front of me and a hand came over mine.

"It's okay, Lillian, they are just pins." Kneeling, she started to help me pick them up, relieved that she didn't yell or strike at me for my mistake. Not that she would. She was always kind and generous towards me.

"See? Nothing to worry about." She assured me as she put the lid back on the container and placed it on the table.

Then she took out her purse and handed me some coins. I counted them and found she gave me more than what I was owed for the week.

"Here, Madam Olgath, you gave me more than what I earned." I held out my hand towards her with the extra coins in my palm, waiting for her to take them back. She gently bent my fingers back over the coins and gave me a soft smile.

"Enjoy yourself at the festival, Lillian. It is my treat."

"Oh, but I couldn't possibly…"

"I'll not hear another word about it. You work hard for my shop and I am pretty sure your gowns are what's keeping this place up and running."

I hugged her and thanked her for her kindness. She smiled at me and motioned towards the door, then stopped and looked at me with raised brows.

"My offer still stands."

"I couldn't possibly intrude." Ever since I've come to work for her, she offered me a permanent place to stay that was away from my father. I knew I couldn't take her up on it because I wouldn't put it past him to search me out. Who knew what damage he would do to the shop if I didn't come home every night? We exited and I placed the coins deep in my pocket, where they were safe for now. Who knows what I would come home to tonight and if the extra coins would only be spent on ale at the local tavern.

I made my way down the street towards the end of town to a small cottage by the woods. I kept my head low and stayed close to the shadows of the tall buildings so no one would see me.

"Hey, Lillian. Where are you going?" I froze at the voice that belonged to Dayton, the blacksmith's son. I quickly picked up my pace, not wanting to interact with him. He was trouble, and I already had enough to deal with at the moment. Suddenly, my arm was yanked backward, and I turned to see the tall young man before me. His grip was firm as he held me in place. I tried to break free, but he only yanked me closer to him the more I resisted.

"I asked you a question." He sneered. He was stronger than most men in our town since he worked alongside his father at the forge.

"Let me go!" I cried, fear shooting through me at his abrasiveness.

"How about a kiss, instead?" He was always making advances on me that I have so far dodged. I tried to yank free again, but he grabbed my other arm and lifted me right up to his face, the local tavern ale wreaked on his breath, and I did my best to face away from him as the stench penetrated my nose.

Suddenly, a sword was at his throat, and we both froze.

"Did you not hear what the lady said?" Came a calm but deadly voice.

I turned and saw the most handsome man I had ever seen. He was tall with short brown hair and piercing blue eyes, which told me this man was dangerous.

His leather attire and dark green cloak were made of fine materials that spoke of wealth and authority. I did not recognize them as any items we sold or made at our little shop, so I knew he was not from around here. Who was this man? I tried to swallow, but it got stuck in my throat as I waited to see what would happen next.

"Don't make me ask again," the stranger hissed to Dayton, who still had not released me from his grip, and was now glaring at the stranger. "Or it will be the last thing you ever do."

At those words, the blacksmith's son slowly set me down on my feet, his grip loosening just enough for me to pull free. I turned and fled the scene before me, running as fast as I could to my little cottage, not even stopping to thank the man who had saved me. I had to get away before Dayton got any more ideas, or if my rescuer decided to follow me. Once I reached the door, I flung it open, grateful my father was not present. I quickly shut the door and put the bolt in place. Once I was safe, I leaned against its frame, grateful a locked door was now between those men and me. My heart was beating out of my chest from what happened.

I could not wait to get away from this town and start a new life elsewhere. What just happened to me was proof that I needed to leave sooner than later. While I was grateful for my work at the seamstress, since it gave me experience and money to help cover any expenses for when I finally did leave, it didn't protect me from my father's wrath or other men in our town who took me for easy prey.

Pushing off the door, I headed upstairs to my room, knelt in front of my bed, and reached underneath it to loosen a board that covered the secret coin pouch I kept beneath it. Pulling out the heavy pouch, I untied the strings that kept it secure and deposited half of my coins in a small bag. I placed the other half in a jar by my bed. I couldn't stash it all away, or my father would become suspicious. Noticing the jar was significantly lower from the last time I got paid told me my father had been in here. He often stole from me to feed his endless thirst for the local tavern ale, which is probably where he was now.

I didn't care.

If he wasn't there, that meant I was free from his wrath which often came in physical punishment. I rubbed my right arm, which was still healing from the last time he came home in a raging, intoxicated fit.

Sighing, I sat on my bed. There was nothing for me in Retna besides Helen and Claira, but they would be gone one day with families of their own, which is why I was preparing now. I was planning to leave within a year since I would be of age and hopefully have enough coins saved by then. If it weren't for my father's greed, I'd probably have enough by now, but the sacrifice of giving him some of my hard-earned wages was worth it if it kept the rest of my earnings safe.

    I got ready for bed and tried to think of tomorrow and our little trio's plans for the festival. With my thoughts on that, I could finally drift off to sleep, but to my surprise, my dreams were occupied by a tall man with piercing blue eyes who saved me today.

Chapter 4

RONIN

He sneered at me as the girl ran away. I lowered my sword once she was farther down the road and out of his reach.

"That was none of your business," he spat, still eyeing my sword.

"It became my business when you grabbed her, and she obviously didn't want your advances."

His face glowed red with anger. I must have hit a nerve, but I wasn't about to let this scum treat that girl with any less dignity than she, or any woman, deserved. For the short time I've been wandering this town, and scouting out the girls I had to pick from tomorrow, it was plain to see women here are treated with far less privilege and dignity than the men were.

When I stopped in the tavern earlier and sat in my corner with my hood down observing what was before me, I was shocked to hear most of the men were hoping their daughters would get chosen. They wanted the enormous bounty that was given to the family if their daughter was picked. It sickened me that these men would trade their own flesh and blood for a few measly coins.

One particular man, who was so drunk he could barely stand with his ale sloshing all over the tavern floor, was going on and on about how he would be glad to get rid of his daughter, even if no coin was given. When he didn't stop there and continued shaming her, I about got up to wrench him by the collar of his shirt and put him in his place. Instead, I walked out of the tavern before I blew my cover, only to find another piece of filth before me now, accosting a young woman. She was frightened, and I knew I had to step in to save the young girl from the brute.

What was wrong with these humans? In Llor, women are treated equally. We worked alongside them as equal partners. They were not treated like cattle to be sold, bartered for, or mistreated at any whim. I was almost glad we had the alliance to help some of these poor girls escape such unfair justice. While I still wasn't keen on getting a wife, I could at least help the one I chose to get an occupation that would pay a fair wage. She could live comfortably in Llor and start a life that she always dreamed of, if that is what she wanted. She would be sorely disappointed if she were hoping for a husband out of the alliance. I would have to choose carefully to ensure she didn't want such a thing from me.

I looked back to the man still leering at me with livid eyes. At least he was wise enough to know when not to pick a fight since he didn't make any move against me. He wouldn't stand a chance even if he did. I was a trained military professional. My skill outdid most fae, so any meager human man was easily taken care of.

"What do you know of my intentions? I only wanted to talk to her." He spat back in my face. I raised my eyebrows and put my hand on the hilt of my sword, challenging him to spew out more lies. I didn't want to make a scene, but I had my honor to uphold. It was my job to protect those in and out of my kingdom; our alliance made it so, even if the monsters we protected them from were their own kind.

He turned on his heel and made his way back to the center of town. I watched him as he entered the blacksmith shop and disappeared from view. I looked back to where the girl had run and saw she was gone. Hopefully, she had made it home safely.

Having had enough of this pitiful town for one day, I opened a portal and headed back to Llor. Leon would get an earful for what I was about to sacrifice, and I would make sure he knew it.

Making my way through the portal, I headed straight toward the training grounds to work off my frustrated emotions. No one would be beating me at a wager today.

Chapter 5

Lillian

I woke up to the sun shining through my window, surprised I was not being pulled out of my bed by my drunken father. That usually meant he stayed at the tavern all night and probably fell asleep at their tables, too drunk to make his way home.

I felt pity for him. He never used to be like this, not until my mother passed away all those years ago from an illness that plagued our little town. He blamed me for not having enough money to care for her needs since they couldn't afford a healer. He was blind to his consumption of ale that took most of our earnings. It only added to his thirst to drown out any memory of her and his failings as a husband and father when she passed away.

The one time I tried to confront him about it left me with a black eye and a broken arm. Since then, I have kept my mouth shut to his ways and tried to avoid him at all costs. Helen and Claira snuck me into their homes on days when he was out of control. I was beyond grateful for my friends who sacrificed so much for me. I would forever be in their debt, even though they did not think of it like that.

I got up and quickly dressed in my working clothes, then checked my father's room to make sure he did not stumble in and fall asleep on his straw mattress early this morning. I had to be extra cautious if he was. Relief swept over me when I noticed his room was empty, and I quickly went about my chores. Heading out to the chicken coop, I gathered the eggs, made my way over to the stall, and milked our cow. Any extra we had, I would sell on market day at the beginning of the week or trade it for items we needed. Then, I made quick work of sweeping and tidying the house. Once I finished, I started a low fire and headed out to the pump to fill up a bucket of water for my bath. Today was the festival, and I wanted to look my best for the activities our little trio had planned for the event.

Soon, I was out the door in a pretty blue dress that had tiny flowers on the design. Something Madam Olgath let me sew in my spare time. I felt it brought out the brown in my eyes along with my complexion. I always had a talent for such things. My mother always complimented me while she was alive, saying I had a knack for matching colors. Something that only grew as I worked at the seamstresses over the last few years. My favorite part was when Claira or Helen would commission a dress, and I got to help them choose the material and fit them to a design that brought out their best features. My heart swelled when they squealed with pleasure every time I showed them their finished gown.

Would they be wearing something I sewed for them at the event? I turned and walked towards the town square, our designated meeting place for today. Usually, we met at the orchards their fathers had a share in, but that would be for later. I heard the fiddler playing in the street and saw children dancing to the music. A smile formed when I saw my dearest friends approaching me.

"Oh, Lillian, I love your dress! Is it new?" Claira asked me enthusiastically as they came up to me. She grabbed my hands and put them out to the side so she could admire my gown.

"Of course she did! Only someone as talented as her could make such a fine gown." Helen beamed at me, then looked at her gown, it was the purple one I gave her yesterday, and she swished it around her legs for emphasis.

My heart filled with pleasure as they complimented me.

"Thank you."

"Well, let's show these beautiful dresses off by dancing, shall we?" Claira declared.

I put my hands behind my back so she couldn't pull me out into the center square where the children danced to the fiddler's songs, lacking her bravery regarding things like this. I was more eager with a needle, thread, and new material that called to be sewn into something exquisite. With my reserved nature, she turned to Helen and dragged her out and onto the dance floor.

Suddenly, a tall man with a lowered hood scooped Helen into his arms and twirled her around. I turned to Claira, seeing if we should interfere, but she came rushing towards me with a smile.

I wondered if it was the same man from earlier. Or one of the fae that came to the festival.

"Well, it seems my dear cousin has an admirer," She giggled.

I turned to ensure she was not signaling us for an intervention, but he lifted her up and twirled her around, a joyous laugh leaving her lips.

My worries about my friend left right as Claira grabbed my hands and twirled me around, using my distraction to her advantage. I could not help the smile that came to my face, even though I didn't like to be the center of attention and was initially hesitant. I could not deny I was having fun twirling around with her. Once we stopped to catch our breath, we turned to find Helen still dancing with the mysterious man.

He didn't look like the man who saved me from Dayton yesterday. This man was more slender and his cloak black, while the man who rescued me was broad, corded with muscle, and wore a dark green cloak. My face flushed, thinking about how handsome the man was who saved me from Dayton's grasp. His brown hair matched mine, but his eyes were a mesmerizing blue. Thinking I should have thanked him for his intervention instead of fleeing the scene. Few people in town would have done that for me since my father was the town drunk. While I was not necessarily shunned, I was often overlooked because of my father's reputation. Most of the town just gave me looks of pity, then went about their business.

"I wonder who he is? He seems captivated by her." Claira said, still smiling in their direction.

"I don't know. I have not seen him before. Have you?"

"No, I have not." Then she gasped and turned to me with bright, wide eyes. "Maybe he's the fae who has come to choose his bride." Her grin went from ear to ear.

"But Helen isn't of age yet, Claira."

"Oh, but to be the bride of a tall and handsome fae." She swooned, her eyes glazing over, stuck in her fantasy.

I giggled and nudged my friend.

"What? Don't you wish to be taken away from here and live a life full of enchantment and…" Then her eyes went wide. "Oh, Lillian! I didn't mean anything by it." Then she pulled me in for a hug and whispered. "If I were a fae, I'd take us all away from here." I returned her hug, knowing she didn't mean any harm. Then, pulling back I grabbed her shoulders gently, and looked straight into her eyes.

"Claira, no fae, no matter how handsome he is, could ever replace my wonderful friendship with you two. Don't worry about me. As long as I have you both, I am more than blessed."

Then I laughed and teased her, "plus, who else could help you choose colors *suitable* for your complexion."

"That was only *one* time, Lillian!"

"Yes, but that yellow was hideous."

Then we laughed together and turned to notice the music had stopped and the man dancing with Helen was still holding her by the waist, not letting go.

More giggles escaped our lips toward our friend and the man besotted with her. This broke their trance, and he immediately let go of Helen's waist, turned, and ran down the alley. We stepped forward to see if we could catch his face behind the hooded cloak or even a name, but he was instantly out of sight. Helen flushed as she made her way back to us, realizing we had been watching her the whole time.

"Who was that?" Claira asked, wiggling her eyebrows.

"I'm not sure. I've never seen him before," Helen replied, turning to look down the alley where the mysterious man had disappeared.

"Hmmm. I wonder? Maybe we will see him tonight at the festival? Let us get going, I'm starving, and we have some baked sweets to eat. Father gave me enough coins to buy for all three of us."

Then she grabbed our hands, and we made our way to the sweet shop for our first treat of the day.

The morning and afternoon went by quickly. Soon, the sun was starting to set, and it was time for us to freshen up for the festival. I bid farewell to Claira and Helen, then headed home to clean up for the upcoming dance.

I looked around, hoping Dayton wasn't nearby. His advances were unwelcome, and I didn't want another encounter like yesterday. When I rejected him a few months ago, his true character was shown by how he treated me. I could not wait to escape this town, my father, and all I had to endure. While I cherished my friendships, it wasn't worth living in fear.

When I was closer to my home, I saw the front door was slightly ajar. I pushed it open slowly to look inside, hoping the wind blew it open and that my father wasn't home yet.

"There you are!" a slurred voice hollered as hands grabbed my arms and jerked me inside. My father flung me towards the table, and I tripped, landing hard on the floor. I turned around to face my drunken father, my body shaking with fear. I wished I hadn't left my friends.

Then he threw the bag of coins I kept hidden under my bed at my feet. The only savings I had to get away from the man before me and start anew was about to be taken from me. I had to blink back tears. The more weakness I showed to my father, the harsher the punishment.

"You lying little minx." He stumbled towards me. I scooted back against the floor, hoping I could escape him.

"You thought you could hide this from me! After all I've done for you!" He yelled, pointing to the bag on the floor.

I stood up to run away, only to be caught by the arm and dragged back. He raised his fist, and I tried to duck, but I wasn't quick enough as pain shot through my eye and the whole side of my face. Everything became a blur as I cried out, putting my hands up to protect myself from any more blows. My head throbbed with pain from his blow.

"That will teach you to never steal from me again!" Then he grabbed my arm and led me out the door. I tried to resist, but my head was spinning so much that I had no choice but to follow him, hoping and praying this was not my end.

Chapter 6

RONIN

It was the night of the festival, and I gathered a few of my men to come with me for protection. You never knew what dark fae prince might show up and cause trouble. My scouts reported that he knew it was Leon's turn to choose a bride from Retna. It will be a surprise when the king doesn't show up, and only a commander is there to claim a bride.

"We'll scout the area once we get there," Caden told me as we headed towards the field to open a portal.

"Thanks, Caden. I know I can rely on you. Prince Devron will surely be there, so keep an eye on them, but don't engage unless they seem like a threat."

"Yes, Commander." He nodded.

Then we opened a portal and stepped through and onto the dirt road outside of the town. The festivities must have started already since music and a mix of voices filled the air. I took a deep breath, wondering what I had wagered for, and signaled my men to spread out and take watch. I knew we intimidated the humans, and it wouldn't help if a small group of fae soldiers showed up to the revelry. It would look more like an attack than a fae who came to claim a bride. I made my way towards the music and hands that clapped to the rhythm of the melody. My eyes constantly scanned the area, and I caught a few dark cloaks hidden in the shadows that notified me the dark fae prince did indeed make it to the festival.

I turned at movement coming from the alleyway and paused when Prince Devron's commander, Nor, stepped out to greet me. The man was taller and broader than most fae, but through many encounters of personally spying on him and the prince, I knew he was an honorable man. Which often confused me as to why he stayed in those dark lands and didn't make his way over to Llor. I would have considered putting him in my army if he had decided to change his allegiance.

I raised my eyebrows at him, surprised he gave away his position to me. He returned it with a smile and stepped forward to greet me, his bare head shining in the moonlight. I quickly scanned the area to make sure this wasn't a trap. I saw nothing but didn't let my guard down.

"Commander Ronin, please be at ease. I've only come to talk with you."

I scoffed at the man who was twice my age. Which was saying something since Fae were immortal.

"What scheme have you and your prince come up with this time, commander? Going to burn down Retna next? Surely, these humans have done nothing to deserve your wrath."

I was surprised that his eyes looked genuinely sad at my words, and he shook his head. I instantly regretted I spoke them to this man.

"No. We are just here to observe, as you probably already know."

I nodded. There was no sense in hiding it. The men under his command were almost as good at scouting as my men were.

"What is it you want?" I asked, getting straight to the point.

Nor turned and looked to the dancing up ahead. I scanned the area and to my surprise, noticed the dark fae prince was dancing with a black-haired beauty. I turned back to Nor, wanting an explanation as to why Prince Devron was openly engaging in the festivities.

He sighed and turned back to me.

"He's not here to ruin your chances for a bride. He met a young girl yesterday and was taken with her. As you can tell, he is now dancing with the fair maiden."

"So, you don't want me to choose her?" I thought about doing the very thing for a moment out of spite for the dark prince, but my character shined through and I knew I would never do such a thing.

"I'm not sure." He sighed. "All I'm asking is that you and your men leave him alone. I promise you are safe, along with the town. I just…he needs…"

I could tell this man cared for his highness, and for some reason, I believed that they were not here to do harm. Then why come at all?

Probably to report back to his brother, the dark fae King.

"You have my word," I told him, hoping to put him at ease.

"Thank you, Commander."

"But, if I see one slip up, I cannot promise anything else."

"Understood." Then he turned and disappeared back into the Alleyway. Not even a shadow signaled he was there, but I knew he wasn't far.

I took a big breath and pondered on what I promised, praying I didn't make a mistake as I made my way to the dance floor, knowing I was about to expose myself as the fae who came to take a bride.

Immediately, all the women turned with eager eyes as they saw me enter. I kept my ears uncovered so it would give me away. The next hour was filled up with dancing around the town's center square as mothers pushed their daughters on me. The current young woman in my arms was a blonde girl named Priscilla, who would not let me get a word in.

"The dress I'm wearing was ordered for this occasion and made specifically for you." She told me while batting her eyelashes. I had to take a deep breath at her undesirable flirting, not wanting to roll my eyes at this young maiden.

"Do you like it?" she asked me. I quickly looked over her gown, noticing it was a mustard yellow and did not match her complexion in the slightest. I was grateful she continued speaking, not giving me a chance to respond. Fae could not lie, so it would be difficult to tell her she looked lovely when in fact she did not.

"The seamstress said it wouldn't enhance my features, but I think I proved her wrong, don't you agree? She was only the assistant anyway."

She should have listened to the seamstress. I only nodded and twirled her to the edge of the makeshift dance floor.

I passed the dark prince a few times by now, but he was so captivated with the girl in his arms I don't even think he noticed me. I kept my promise and did not intervene or demand why he was here. So far, his commander's words were proving true, and he was only here for the young girl currently in his arms.

I heard a commotion to my right, and I shifted my eyes to see who was making the racket. My breath caught when I saw the same girl I saved yesterday, only she was now with an older man who had a firm grip on her upper arm. I turned to the girl in my arms.

"Excuse me. It seems my attention is needed."

"Oh, but…"

I didn't let her finish and immediately made my way through the couples dancing toward the girl. The closer I got, I noticed the young maiden's eye was swollen and starting to bruise. It looked fresh since her eyes were also glistening with tears. The offense wasn't there when I helped her yesterday, and rage rose in my body at whoever did this to her. Probably the man who was now gripping her arm and shaking her.

It would seem I have found my bride.

Chapter 7

LILLIAN

"Stand up straight!" My father hissed at me. I was hiding my face from everyone around me, embarrassed about my swollen eye that was no doubt bruised already. He turned, blocking me from anyone's view, grabbed my arm, and shook me. I became nauseous, and my head throbbed with pain as he throttled my body. No one could see what was happening since the sun had already set, and the only light came from the paper lanterns hanging from the rope above us.

"I'd have been rid of you by now if you weren't so ugly. Now, I'm only burdened with an ungracious daughter who will torment me the rest of my days."

I should have been used to his criticism, but the words still stung and burrowed deep in my heart. I would never be good enough for him, no matter how many times my friends told me his words were a lie.

"Touch her again, and we'll see who has the next strike." A deep voice to my right said, and I slightly turned, not wanting him to see my swollen eye since I recognized him as the man who saved me yesterday. Embarrassment shot through me that he had to intervene on my part constantly.

"Who do you think you are? I'm her father, you scoundrel. Leave us alone!"

Suddenly, the man placed himself between my father and me, acting as a shield from the cruel man who raised what he thought was a worthless daughter. For the first time in a long time, I felt safe.

"It seems I will be relieving you of that title, you scum! How dare you touch a woman, especially those under your protection."

"I said leave us alone!" I saw my father's arm reach around the man to grab me, but the large man quickly grabbed him by the front of his shirt and lifted my father up to his face. His other arm bent backward to keep me close to his body in a protective stance.

"Do you know who I am, you wretched man! You should be grateful I don't end you right now!" He hissed up at my father, whose eyes were now wide with fear.

"You're...you're..." my father wheezed, "...a fae!"

I was shocked at my father's words and looked up to notice pointed ears that stuck out on the side of my rescuer's head, his short hair making it all the more visible. I slightly turned to look at my father and noticed silver wisps were around the fae's hand that held my father high off the ground. While I hated him, I didn't want him to die.

"Please, sir." I put my hand on the fae's arm, hoping to ease his anger. It was a risk, but I was willing to take it.

He turned to me, his blue eyes blazing with rage. Then they softened as he scanned my face and slowly let my father down from his grasp. At the last moment, he threw him down onto the stone-paved street, where he grunted in pain.

I looked around, and some of the townsfolk had stopped dancing and were observing us with wide eyes and hushed whispers.

The fae turned back to me and gently placed his arms on either side of my shoulders, looking at me with pity. I didn't want his pity, I just wanted to feel safe.

Then he raised his head and scanned over the audience now facing our way. I tucked my chin to my chest, letting my hair fall in front of my face to hide my swollen eye.

"I have found my bride." He called to the crowd.

I jerked my head up to look at him. He couldn't be talking about me, could he? I was still a month away from becoming of age, and he could not possibly want a girl who was beaten and bruised. I didn't come even close to the other beauties here tonight. Then he placed a hand around my waist and pulled me to his side. His other hand motioned for me to proceed through the crowd. I searched his eyes, making sure I didn't misunderstand. They were full of compassion this time. As he gave me a small smile, I knew he was serious about what he had said.

"This way, my lady." His soft words were a balm to my broken heart. Then fear filled me. I've never been anywhere besides Retna, and my plans for leaving were still far off. To go to the fae lands that were so foreign to me made me wonder if I should tell him to find another bride. Someone more worthy of his time and affection.

"Wait!" My father yelled behind us. We both turned and noticed he was struggling to get up. My resolve to stay immediately dissolved.

"What about the bounty you owe me for her!"

The fae protecting me scoffed and turned us back around to continue our way.

"Wait! You owe me! It's part of the alliance!"

The man stopped and put me behind his back again.

"I will say this only once, you piece of filth. You will never see a single piece of *her* dowry.

Now, nor ever. Your payment is me sparing your life."

Then he turned back around and I almost squealed as he bent and picked me up in his arms. He had one hand on my back and the other under my knees. I've never been this close to a man before, or held in such an intimate manner. My face flushed as his warmth seeped into my cold body, providing comfort in both a physical and emotional form. I wrapped my hands around his neck as he swiftly cut his way through the crowd that was now quiet. Maybe being chosen wouldn't be so bad after all.

Chapter 8

RONIN

I don't know what overcame me to pick the girl up in my arms, but my heart pounded in my chest at her nearness, and I couldn't seem to put her down. Seeing her vulnerability back there brought out a fierce protection for her that surprised me, especially when I saw her black eye. I still wasn't planning on actually making her my bride, but I needed to get her away from her cruel father.

Having her in my arms assured me that she was at least safe from the man, and bringing her to Llor would ensure it stayed that way. I would talk to Leon about getting her an occupation in the village outside the castle where I could keep an eye on her.

No. I couldn't do that. I needed to get her on her feet, then be done with the lass. I didn't have time to worry about this young maiden with beautiful dark brown hair whose arms were wrapped around my neck and clinging to me for dear life.

I scanned the woods we were about to enter and saw my men making their way towards me. Shock was in their eyes and faces as they noticed the young woman in my arms.

"Everything okay?" My captain asked as he stopped before me, eyes scanning the girl in my arms.

"We must get her back to the castle as soon as possible. She's hurt," I told him quickly.

He nodded and opened a portal to Llor, and my men stepped through.

I looked down at the girl, who raised her wide eyes to me. My heart clenched that they were full of fear, hoping it wasn't from me since I would never hurt her. I Slowly put her down, then grabbed her hands to keep her attention. She searched my face, not saying a word. Looking over to the portal and then back to the town.

I took a big breath to calm my nerves. She needed to know the situation to the fullest in case she didn't want to go to Llor once she discovered my intentions.

"I need you to know I never planned on taking a bride." Her eyes went wide and she pulled her hands out from mine. I immediately missed the feel of them and about snatched them back into mine own, realizing my actions could be mistaken for aggression, so I clenched my fists instead as I watched her look around the forest for an escape. I cleared my throat, grabbing her attention to quickly explain since I didn't want her returning to the town and the wretched man she called father.

"Please, do not be frightened. It has nothing to do with you, it is only that I am the Commander of the entire army of the Kingdom of Llor, and my duties do not allow for much freedom, but if you wish to go with me..." I stepped closer to her and gently grabbed her chin between my thumb and finger, tilting it up until our gazes met. Her eye was so swollen, and fierce protectiveness surged through me once more. I about withdrew my sword and stomped back to Retna to finish the job I threatened her father with.

No. She needed me here. The man could rot for all I care.

"I can promise you safety and comfort. The dowry that was supposed to be given to your father; will all go to you. You will never want for anything ever again, and if you so desire, I can even find you an occupation within our kingdom that suits your needs."

I watched her thoughts swirl in her eyes, contemplating my offer. Then she nodded. Relief swept through me that I didn't have to force her to come back with me to Llor since I refused to allow her to go back to that cruel town and its men who had no honor. Releasing her, I gently grabbed her hand to help her through the portal. I felt a tug on my fingers and turned back towards her.

"Thank you," she softly said, "but I must ask you something before we go." She looked hesitant at the swirling portal of colors before her, then back to me. "I am excellent with a needle and was an assistant to the seamstress here before you…" she paused, "do you have any need for those where you live?"

My thoughts turned back to the girl in the mustard yellow dress. She must have been the assistant who tried to steer the girl from the wretched color. I smiled inwardly and looked over the timid girl before me. I would find her the same occupation even if I had to do a little manipulation to the king himself. He got me in this mess anyway.

I would also talk with my captain. His wife was also human and an assistant to Madam Serale, the seamstress of Llor. I was sure it would help the situation and hopefully bring a sense of familiarity to the girl to have another human around. Caden volunteered over twenty years ago to pick a bride. While he was eager to do so, I was not.

"Yes, we do. I will personally talk with the King and Madam Serale to get you work, if that is what you wish?"

A smile formed on her face for the first time tonight, and my breath caught in my chest. It gave me joy to help her, and seeing her smile gave me satisfaction that filled my whole body.

"Yes, that would be wonderful. Thank you. My name is Lillian, Commander."

For some reason, I didn't want her to address me by my title.

"Ronin."

She smiled again and nodded. "Thank you, Ronin."

I liked hearing my name on her lips.

No. I did not have time for this.

I had duties to my kingdom and I could not get tangled with this girl. I would talk to Leon tonight, the sooner she was taken care of and out of my sight, the better for both of us, I tried to persuade myself.

Then, we stepped through the portal together to catch up with my men.

Chapter 9

LILLIAN

Going through the portal was like stepping through a waterfall, refreshing as a tingle swept over my body. We stepped out of the swirling mist and in front of the largest and most majestic building I have ever seen. Its white stone spires were smooth as they shot up and faded into the night sky. The stars glowing around it only made the castle more ethereal. Large lanterns lit the entire courtyard, shining upon beautiful wooden doors with an intricate design around the edge that had to be the entrance.

He gently took my hand, and made our way up the large stone steps that curved around the door. Everything here was perfection, nothing out of place. I looked around as he led me along. I could see flowers of every color in the distance as the moonlight graced their petals. I couldn't wait to explore the castle grounds. It was like a dream being here, and I was caught up in the moment.

"This way, Lillian." I turned to Ronin, not realizing I had stopped. I was so mesmerized by my surroundings that I couldn't help but stare. I flushed at being caught gaping at what was before me. What must he think of me? This was his normal everyday life, while mine was full of fear. *No, not anymore, though.* I looked back to where we stepped through the portal and saw it was now gone. A sinking feeling entered my chest, and reality hit me that I was no longer in Retna. Claira and Helen were so far away now. They must be worried sick for me. They were my only source of strength, friendship, and happiness in that town, and now they were far away and out of reach.

I turned back to Ronin, his brows pulled down in what looked like concern. I was so grateful to him, even if he didn't want me as a bride, which gave me some relief, but if I was honest, it also stung a little. No man ever wanted me, and those who did were less than respectful. Finally, when I met a man who not only saved me once but twice from men who would use and abuse me, he wanted nothing to do with me. I couldn't help the sigh that left me.

"Is everything alright?" He stepped closer, and his warmth seeped into me as I looked up at this tall, masculine fae before me. He was the most handsome man I have ever seen. His pointed ears only added to his beauty, and I wanted to touch them for some reason. I shook my thoughts. He didn't want me, but I would try my hardest to be positive and grateful for the opportunities he was about to give me: money and work. I could start a new life here, like I planned. Maybe fate was truly on my side. I gave him the biggest smile I could muster, to which he returned.

"Yes, Ronin. I'm just overwhelmed and grateful for the opportunity to be here. Sorry for stopping. Please, lead the way."

He didn't move but looked over me again, stopping on my face. His brows pinched together, and I put my hand up to touch the swollen skin around my eye as gently as I could. Pain seared the area, and I realized it was worse than I thought.

He didn't say anything but grabbed my hand and started walking again. For a man who was determined to leave me be, he held my hand a lot. Maybe fae were more friendly than humans and it meant nothing.

I wouldn't give any weight to his gestures. He made sure to let me know that he wasn't in search of a bride.

Instead of leading me through the magnificent doors before us, he veered to the right to a small entryway. He opened the door, and we entered a brightly lit area that looked like a medical ward. Unoccupied beds were on one side, and many shelves full of herbs and concoctions were on the other.

"Please sit." He pointed to the bed. I sat down at the edge clasping my hands in my lap to prevent them from fidgeting.

"Healer Tueron, are you here?" he called out.

An older fae shortly made his way into the room. He wore long gray robes over a tunic and pants. His black hair was peppered with gray as he wore it in the short style, like Ronin's. Spectacles were at the edge of his nose, and a quick smile on his face. He had a friendly demeanor.

"Yes, commander. Does one of your men need attention?" He must not have noticed my eye. It made sense. He probably knew the commander was taking a bride today and maybe thought one of his men got hurt on my behalf. It was confirmed when Ronin motioned towards me.

The man looked at me more thoroughly this time, and his eyes became wide and almost angry.

"Oh, dear. What happened? You poor girl." Then he turned to the commander with raised brows and an accusatory scowl.

"Do explain why a woman is in my clinic with a swollen and bruised eye? I thought you went to get a bride?" He grabbed a stool, sat in front of me, and lifted my chin to examine my face.

"It wasn't him!" I quickly interjected, not wanting him to think the commander had anything to do with my current state. The healer turned back to me, and his features softened as he softly spoke.

"Of course not, my dear. Our commander here is too honorable and loyal. I didn't mean to shame his name and cause offense." Then he gave me a soft smile. "So, what *did* happen?"

I was hesitant at first, but realized my father was not here and I was not going back home and that seemed to give me the courage to tell him about my father's rage.

"Does anywhere else hurt?" He asked after I quickly explained my black eye.

I looked to Ronin, who nodded at me, giving me the courage to continue.

"Yes." I pointed to my arm, where my father's firm grip left my skin tender. He lifted up my sleeve and we both saw spots of blue and black along my arm where his fingers dug into my skin.

Looking up at the healer to see his reaction, I saw his lips pinched with worry. He nodded to me and got up to go to the shelf full of herbs. I watched as he put leaves and some kind of paste in a bowl, then mixed them together. Movement caught my eye and I noticed Ronin was turned away from me, his fist clenched at his sides.

"It's okay, Ronin. It doesn't hurt." Trying to comfort him. My heart swelled that this man who barely knew me, was showing so much concern for my well-being.

He turned to look at me but the healer cut him off as he stepped back in front of me and started to carefully put a salve over my bruises and eye. It felt cool and refreshing, and I was surprised when the pain began to ease after only a few seconds.

"This will help bring down the swelling and enhance the healing. Apply twice daily, once in the morning and at night before you go to bed. Within a couple of days it should be back to normal."

"Thank you," I told the fae as he handed me the small jar. "How can I ever repay you?" I realized all my coins were back in Retna, and since it was in my father's grasp, there probably wouldn't be any left for very long.

"Don't worry dear, it's part of my job at the castle." He winked at me and turned back to the Commander. "You'll be taking care of her then?"

"Yes."

"Good. It seems my work here is finished since you're in good hands. The Commander takes care of his men and anyone in his charge."

I was grateful for the assurance, not that I ever doubted Ronin's honor but it was nice to hear it from someone else. Thanking him once more, we exited a different door connecting to the rest of the castle instead of the one we entered from. It was quiet as we walked down the large, expansive hallway. Everything was built with white marble, including the floors and the pillars that lined the hallway. The arches between each pillar seemed to be laden with gold. It spoke of wealth and had a sense of enchantment to it.

After a few moments, we stopped in front of another large set of doors and Ronin knocked.

"Come in." came a voice from behind the door. He opened it and motioned for me to enter ahead of him. I looked down at the jar I was holding in my hands, then up at Ronin. He gave me a reassuring smile.

"It's just King Leon."

Just the king? I know I looked a sight to see and was hoping it would be a few days before we talked to his majesty about my situation. A few days to allow this salve to work its miracle.

"He's going to help you. I promise," he assured me.

Not that I doubted him, I was only hoping to get a chance to look more presentable. I took a deep breath and put on the best smile I could, since there was no other choice. "Okay."

Then I stepped through the threshold with the commander's hand on my back, which not only gave me a thrill, but the encouragement I needed.

Chapter 10

RONIN

If anything, Lillian was brave. She went through so much in such a short time. This wasn't the ideal situation for taking a bride, but I was trying to soothe her as much as I could, granted the situation. I initially was going to take her to Leon first, but I knew she was in pain and decided to get her the help she needed before pleading our case to his majesty. When I saw the bruises on her arm in addition to her eye, I had to turn away to prevent her from seeing the rage that was bubbling up inside of me.

"Ronin! Tell me…" Leon stopped short once he saw Lillian. His eyes went wide as they moved back and forth from me to her. Then, catching himself, he put on a smile and came forward, giving me a look that demanded an explanation of the girl's current condition.

"Later." I quietly told him, and he gave a slight nod to tell me he heard and understood. I stepped to the side of Lillian and tugged her close to me, wanting her to feel safe.

"This is Lillian, Your Majesty." I turned to her, and she pulled away from my grasp. Maybe I was overstepping my bounds, but relief came when I realized she only needed space to give my friend a curtsy.

"Your Majesty." She quickly spoke, then to my relief, she tucked herself right back under my arms. When my heart swelled with pleasure, I pushed it down.

"Welcome to Llor, Lillian. I am King Leon and it would seem you are the lucky girl to have caught my commander's…"

"Actually, Your Majesty, our situation is a little different." I cut off my friend before he made the situation any more awkward for all of us.

"Oh, I see." He continued smiling at us as if nothing was wrong, but I knew he would demand answers later. "Well, how may I be of service then."

"Lillian is very tired and has had a trying day. I was hoping you had a room to spare for the next while until I get her comfortable and situated."

"That can be arranged." Then he called out "Wilson!" A tall fae stepped through the door and into the study. It was as if he was waiting for his majesty's command. He wore a gray tunic and pants lined with embroidery. He bowed deeply once he was right in front of his majesty.

"Yes, Your Majesty?"

"See that Lady Lillian is taken care of." He told the servant, gesturing to the girl beside me.

"Yes, Your Majesty." Then he held out an arm to her, but instead of taking it, she turned to me.

"He'll take care of you, Lillian. I'll make sure to check on you tomorrow. I need to talk with his highness about our arrangement." She nodded and then turned to Leon.

"Thank you, Your Majesty, for everything."

"It is my pleasure. I look forward to meeting you again." Then he stepped forward, looked at me with raised eyes, then picked up her hand and kissed it with a smile on his face.

An emotion surged through me that I didn't quite understand. It was anger and shock all at the same time, but not the same kind of anger I had when I saved her this evening. I wanted to yank her hands away from his lips, but I knew I could not do such a thing since I had no real reason to do so. I've never been jealous before, but that was the only way I could explain the emotions that were swelling within me.

This was ridiculous. Since when did I ever become jealous? I barely knew this girl and I had many women who wanted my attention, so why was she so different? I wouldn't let him see how it affected me, so I turned the other way with a straight face as if nothing bothered me.

"Goodbye, Ronin." I quickly turned back to Lillian and saw she had a smile for me, and my nerves settled. At least, that is what I hope it was for and not from the kiss my friend bestowed upon her. I also noticed her eye was already healing, and I knew I did the right thing by bringing her here.

She turned to leave with the tall fae through the door and I almost followed to make sure she was taken care of, even though I knew she would be.

"Ronin, I need you to explain why this girl is not your bride, *and* why she looks as if she was dragged through the streets!"

I sighed and turned to my best friend, explaining everything that happened within the last couple of hours, from how I found her beaten and bruised, to her father and the promises I gave her.

"I don't even know if she is of age yet, but I couldn't leave her there."

"You were always the honorable one, but that could be a problem. I know humans are particular about age since their lives are so short. I'm grateful you brought her back here, and I will do all I can to make sure she is comfortable."

"Thank you, Leon. I knew I could trust you."

"Not a problem. I am curious though, what if she *is* of age? Why not marry her?"

"No."

"I know our wager was out of jest and I never should have made you follow through with it, but Ronin, I am not blind. I saw the way you looked at her and protected her." Then a wicked gleam came into his eyes, "especially when I kissed her hand." I rolled my eyes at him and scoffed. He only chuckled.

"She is very pretty. Maybe you should rethink this situation." He continued.

"I can't Leon. My duties are to you and the Kingdom. I don't feel that way towards her. I just need to make sure she is taken care of, and things will go back to normal. I would be grateful if you could talk to Madam Serale on behalf of the girl."

"I'll do that." He sighed as if defeated, but I felt this was not over yet for some reason.

"Thank you."

"What about the dowry?" He asked.

"I refuse to give it to her father, not after how he treated her. That man can rot in prison for all I care." I almost asked if I could do that very thing, but we didn't have jurisdiction over that town, which could bring a whole set of problems, so I bit my tongue.

"I understand why, but I'll have to settle things between Retna to keep our alliance strong." Then he gave me a pointed look. "Ronin, it's a good thing I like you."

Then he smiled at me while shaking his head back and forth, a chuckle escaping his lips. I joined him knowing I caused him a headache sometimes, but I was grateful that he understood. He was not just my closest friend, almost like a brother, but he was a great leader and king to our people. I was proud to serve him.

"I was hoping we could give the dowry to her instead. That way she can start over and make a life for herself in Llor."

"I think that's a wonderful idea. Once she is settled, I'll make sure she gets the full amount owed."

"Thank you, Leon, for everything."

He clapped me on the shoulder and motioned towards a seat. I slightly shook my head at him.

"I have to find my captain. His wife is assistant to Madam Serale, and I want to put in a good word for Lillian before I speak with the seamstress tomorrow."

"She's human, too, if I recall correctly."

"Yes, I believe he was chosen about twenty years ago to pick a bride."

Leon smirked, "He wasn't chosen. He begged me to pick him."

"Really?"

"Yes." Then he raised his eyebrows to me and gave me a broad grin, "and look how happy he is with a *human* wife at his side."

"I'm leaving." I turned and headed towards the door with his majesty's laughter echoing into the halls. I had a captain to find, not a bride to take.

Chapter 11

LILLIAN

The fae named Wilson led me down the expansive halls. The candles and bulbs that shimmered in the air lit up the hallway, showing its grandeur. We walked down the center on a dark maroon carpet that muffled our steps on the white, marbled floors below it. The hallway went on for as far as the eye could see.

Paintings and statues of fae were placed evenly down the walls on either side of us. Most of the art depicted beautiful gardens and fae playing instruments surrounded by animals of every kind. We turned to the right once we reached the end of the hall and went up a broad staircase that curved to a second floor. The handrails seemed to be made of crystal and the knobs silver. I felt so out of place here, but soon I would be back in a village, even if it was a fae one, and all would be right with the world.

He opened the door to my left and motioned for me to enter.

"I'll be right back with some maids to attend to you," he bowed.

"Thank you," I returned with a curtsy, hoping none of my actions were offending or too much.

Fae culture was so different from humans.

He nodded and headed back down the hall, leaving me to myself. I turned around to see what kind of room I had been assigned to, and it stole the very breath from my lungs.

It was so large that my home would have fit into the entire chamber. It had a large four-poster bed in the center with light blue coverings. Sheer white material flowed down each post and connected at the top, making it look like a waterfall. Fresh flowers were on the side table, and the carpet was so plush it felt like walking on clouds. A small fire was burning in the stone hearth to my left, and another door was to my right. I didn't know what was behind it, but I was sure I'd find out soon enough.

Turning to the sound of the door being pushed open, I saw three maids enter carrying baskets in their arms. They all wore the same gray material as the fae who led me here, except they were in gowns and a white apron placed around their middle, a white cap on their head.

"Oh, my poor dear." Said the tallest fae, who had brown hair, sparkling green eyes, and looked to be only a few years older than me- They all did. She hurried to me and looked me over. I tucked my head, flushing at the unwanted attention. I knew I looked awful with my bruises and shaken countenance.

Suddenly, her hands were over mine. I looked up at her to see a smile on her face and pinched brows as if to apologize for whatever happened to me. Her compassion almost broke my composure since I had already received so much of it today.

"Leave the lass alone, Myra." Said the shorter of the three. She had blonde hair and was busy putting the basket near the door.

The third maid came up to me, whose hair was as rich as honey, and put her hand on my arm.

"She meant nothing by it, Celia." She said, turning to the maid by the door, then turned back to me and reached for the jar that was grasped in my hands that I reluctantly let her have. She patted my arm and set it on the edge of the stand next to the bed. Then coming back to me she put an arm around my waist and led me to the door where Celia entered with Myra following behind her.

"My name is Martha, and as you now know, that is Myra and Celia." She told me nodding to the other two.

"Nice to meet you. My name is Lillian."

"Such a pretty name. Now, let's get you all cleaned up and ready for bed. Where are your clothes? Myra will put them away for you and get your nightgown ready."

Panic went through me. I didn't even think about such things when we left Retna. I was so caught up in the moment of all that happened that packing necessities didn't even dawn on me.

"I didn't bring anything, I'm sorry. We were in such a rush to leave that I didn't have a chance to grab anything."

"Oh, you must be Ronin's new human bride, then." She beamed. "Don't tell me the commander gave you that?" she said, pointing to my eye, almost skeptically.

"Oh no! He's been nothing but a gentleman!" I rushed to defend him. "In fact, he saved me, but I am not his bride."

"You're not? Then who did he pick?" Mrya came up to us with eagerness.

"No one. We came to some sort of arrangement."

"Really? He's so handsome, though." She swooned and sat on the bed, holding a towel to her chest, and sighed with a grin.

"Quiet, Myra. Get back to your duties." Celia snapped from inside the door. I looked towards her and noticed a large bathtub was being filled with steamy water, and I longed to soak in it.

"It's true though. Almost every woman swoons over that man, but he refuses to give any one of us a chance." She ended with a pout. "Believe me, I've tried. It's like we aren't worth his time."

"He is busy protecting this kingdom and doesn't have time for any of your silliness." Celia hollered back. For some odd reason, their words gave me comfort that I wasn't the only woman he rejected. It wasn't just me that he didn't want, it was the notion of marriage and his duty to his kingdom that left him single.

"Quiet, you two! It's none of our business what the commander does or does not do. Now hush and let us help this young girl get ready for bed, she has had a long day." Martha scolded the two young maids, who turned red with her reprimand and nodded to her.

"Now, I'll be back in a jiffy with some clothes for you." She took some hand measurements, nodded to herself, and then left the room.

"Come this way," Myra said, motioning me towards the bath. The water was warm, and it felt so good to wash away the grime and worries of the day. The scented oils smelled so fresh and lovely that I didn't want to leave.

Martha came back with an armful of gowns and all sorts of necessities a young lady needed. It felt odd, to say the least, when they helped me dress for bed. I never had a handmaiden before, and the dresses I did have were sewn by myself, so I could add buttons along the front to make it easier for me to get on and off.

"There. You look so lovely now, and your eye is practically healed."

"Really?"

"Yes, take a look." Celia brought over a mirror from the vanity and I looked at my eye. It was no longer swollen and the bruising was a pale blue and black.

"Healer Tueron is a miracle worker around here, especially for the humans who dwell in Llor.

You are so fragile compared to fae, unless you are bonded to one."

"Are there a lot of humans in Llor?" I knew a bride was chosen every five years, but that couldn't be enough to change their population.

"Not too many since most become bonded, but a few stragglers find our land and stay. Our king is just and fair, which makes living here all the better." Martha replied.

"Bonded? What's that?"

"Oh, you know, the ritual that binds you to your mate?" Myra sighed with a dreamy look. "I can't wait to be bonded."

"Like marriage?"

"I guess that is what it would be in human terms, but it's so much more than that." I was surprised that Celia was the one who responded to my question.

"Celia was recently bonded to her mate, Trent." Myra interjected. "It was so beautiful, the flowers, and the whole ritual that is performed."

"There's a ritual too?"

"Oh, yes. It binds you to them and creates a soul-deep connection that is so pure and beautiful." She continued.

"That's enough talk, it's getting late, and the Lady needs her sleep," Martha told the maids. I realized Martha was the leader of their small group as the other two nodded and followed her out the door. Myra and Celia turned to me, smiling, which I returned before they softly closed the door behind them.

I did not want them to go, but I knew it was late. I was intrigued about this ritual that bound people together and wanted to learn more about it. Llor wasn't only a different place but a whole realm. Magic ruled these lands, and I couldn't wait to discover all that it had to offer.

Making my way to the large bed, I pulled back the thick covers and slid in. I've never slept on something so soft. I looked around at the floating lights, wondering how to blow them out or dim them so I could get some much-needed rest. It seemed as if they could read my mind since right after I thought about how I would go about doing the task, they dimmed themselves, leaving a soft, comfortable glow to fall asleep to. Closing my eyes, I instantly fell into a dreamless sleep, hoping that it wasn't a dream when I woke up.

Chapter 12

RONIN

I woke up early and made my way to the training field where my captain usually was. He was ambitious like me and trained constantly. I trusted him more than most and hoped he could assist me by getting Lillian acquainted with his wife and the seamstress.

Dust was flying in the air as I came up to the training grounds and noticed he was already training with some of my men. They shuffled their feet back and forth, blocking and stabbing their opponent with great skill.

"Caden!" I called out to him from the sidelines. He raised his hand to Drew, one of my knights he was currently fighting, then turned and made his way over to me. He looked around as if searching for something.

"Where's the girl?"

"Lillian? The one I brought back yesterday?"

"Yes. How's she doing? Is her eye better?"

"I took her to the healer, and I'm on my way to fetch her from her room, but first, I need a favor."

He nodded for me to continue.

"Your wife is human, right?"

He grinned at my inquiry."Yes, why? Are you changing your mind and want to marry the girl?"

"No." Why was everyone assuming I wanted to marry? Most of my men knew my desire to be free of such chains.

"I don't understand?"

"Well, Lillian said she used to be an assistant to a seamstress in Retna, and if I remember correctly, your wife is an assistant to Madam Serale?"

"She is. Do you want me to help her find work with Madam Serale?"

"Yes, and maybe your wife could befriend the girl. Give her a sense of normality here. I've already talked to the King, and she practically has the job, but I want her to feel welcomed since she's been through so much already."

My captain's eyebrows raised. "If I didn't know any better, Commander, I'd say you were fond of this girl. I have never once seen you help a female as much as you are doing now. In fact, you're usually pushing away their advances."

"Don't be ridiculous, Caden. I help many people. It's our duty to the kingdom and its subjects."

"I know, but this is different. Isn't it?" His sly grin hinted at something that was outrageous.

"Enough. First the king, now you! Did he put you up to this? Can't a man just be honorable without intending to actually shackle himself down to some maiden?"

He returned my outburst with a laugh. These men were infuriating!

"I don't know. I like being shackled." His eyes glowing with humor.

I snorted.

"Anyway, can you help me?"

"Of course. I'll quickly change and see my wife and Madam Serale to let them know the situation. No doubt the king has already sent a letter?"

"Yes, this morning."

"I'll meet you at the seamstresses then."

"See you soon."

I turned and headed toward the doors that led into the castle, only to find Lillian coming out of them with two servants following right behind her. They held a small chest in each of their hands that hopefully was filled with items for Lillian. In our rush to leave, I didn't think about going and grabbing her clothes or the precious trinkets she needed for living here. I would take her back to Retna to gather her items if she asked me to, and I would make sure to offer. The thought of seeing her father again made my blood boil.

I looked at her eyes to see how it fared, noticing it was practically healed, to my great relief. I continued to look over the rest of her to ensure there were no more injuries and saw she wore a dark green dress in the style of the fae that gracefully and modestly hugged her curves.

A giggle came from one of the maids, and I shot my eyes up to them, realizing I got caught gaping at her. Lillian's face was red from my examination, and I was sure mine matched. So much for looking at her injuries.

Clearing my throat and trying to brush off my actions, I asked her how her morning went and if she was taken care of.

"Yes, thank you so much for all you are doing. I received a note early this morning to be ready since we were meeting with Madam Serale."

"Yes, I'm glad you got it. I spoke with my captain, whose wife also works at the seamstresses, and he will be informing them of our arrival."

"I hope it won't be too much trouble. If so, I'm sure I can find work somewhere else."

"No trouble at all. I'm glad to help in any way I can. Plus, the king owes me a favor." After what I've been through, he owed me more than that. "Let us be on our way."

"Yes. I'm looking forward to meeting them. Thank you." Then she turned to take the chest from the maids.

"Allow me." I stepped forward, and the tallest of them, whose hair was a lighter brown than Lillian's, stared at me with dreamy eyes and gave me a wink as she handed me the small chest. I gave her a curt nod, trying to disregard her flirtations while trying not to be rude. Grabbing it by the handle, I quickly turned, taking the other one from the other maid, who was rolling her eyes at her friend. I was used to this kind of thing from Fae and other women in the village, but I made sure to keep it known that I was not in search of a mate. Not now, not ever. It didn't stop them from trying though. Sometimes, they were so forward I had to be more blunt when their actions led to impropriety. Luckily, this wasn't one of those occasions.

I turned back to Lillian, whose eyebrows were raised and looking between the maid who winked at me and then back to myself. Her reaction almost made me smile when I thought I caught a bit of jealousy being tampered down behind her eyes. She had nothing to worry about, but I wasn't about to say that out loud. I held out my elbow for her to grab. Even though I was carrying the chest, it was small width-wise, which allowed me some room to make the offer. I told myself it was to prove that I was doing my knightly duty to help the lady along and not to show the maid I was already taken. No, not taken, just not interested in anyone. It was too late to retract my offer, and I inwardly sighed at the situation I put her in since she turned to the maid who flirted, then back to me, hesitantly looking at my arm. Needing her to know that I was not interested in the maid and she had nothing to worry about, I moved my elbow closer to her.

"Let's go, Lillian, Madam Serale awaits us, and I have a prompt reputation to uphold." I nudged my arm for her to take.

"Sorry, Commander."

"Ronin."

"Ronin." She smiled up at me and thankfully took my arm. Looking down at her small hand wrapped around the crook of my arm filled my chest with pleasure that shot all the way through my body.

We walked quickly down the paved cobblestone streets that ran through the entire city. Shops were open with fae and humans bustling back and forth along the road. Stands full of fresh vegetables and fruit were for sale from local farmers along with household items from the carpenters, among other things. Everyone was friendly, and many waved as we passed by. I knew Llor was ten times larger than Retna, and I looked to Lillian to see how she was handling the vast difference. I was grateful when I saw her eyes filled with wonder and amazement.

"Do you like it?"

"It's so big and full of life. So different from Retna. I'm sure I'll enjoy living here."

"I'm so glad to hear that."

She smiled at me, and I almost wished I would have taken her as my mate, but that thought quickly came then left.

"Commander! Commander Ronin!"

We both turned, and I saw Tristan running toward us. He stopped right in front of me and put his hands on his knees, trying to catch his breath.

"Hello, Tristan. What brings you out here?"

The Young boy pointed behind him, and I saw the stablemaster negotiating with another fae who had a horse in his hands.

"My father is trying to get another mare for the stables. I guess she has good breeding stock, whatever that means." He said, flicking his hand in the air as if it wasn't important. Chuckling at his ignorance, I ruffled his hair.

"Then I saw you and the pretty lady and came to say hi. Is she the one you lost the wager to?" He asked eagerly.

I froze at his words as heat crept into my cheeks from embarrassment. I never wanted Lillian to know the reason I was chosen to pick a bride. Losing a wager to the king was not something to boast about, especially when I wasn't fulfilling the bet I got conned into participating. Not daring to turn and look at her reaction, I gave him a reprimanded look instead. He seemed not to have noticed since his next words only added to my mortification. I would have to speak to him later about proper etiquette along with a sword fighting lesson; it seemed both were greatly needed.

"If so, I'm glad you lost! She's beautiful, commander!"

I didn't know how to respond. She was, but we were both about to move on with our lives, and I couldn't have any connections to her, words or otherwise.

Then a glorious laugh filled my ears, and I turned to see Lillian step in front of the boy.

"You are so sweet? What is your name?"

"Tristan!" he beamed up at her.

"Well, Tristan, the commander and I have come to some sort of arrangement which suits us both equally." She turned and patted my arm, giving me a reassuring smile, then turned back to the stableboy.

"Oh, so you didn't marry him?" His countenance became sad as he looked between us.

"No." She chuckled. "But, he is the noblest man I have ever met, and I hope you are learning from him."

"Oh, yes! He's teaching me how to fight." Then he jabbed the air with his fist as if he had a sword and was blocking an enemy.

We both laughed, and he beamed up at us. Glad she was taking this situation and turning it around. I was worried about how she would react to his words.

"Marvelous! You are almost better than the commander!" She praised him, and I about rolled my eyes.

"Really? You think so?"

"If you keep practicing, I know you'll be just as good as him one day."

"Oh, boy!" Then he turned to me, "I am glad you didn't marry her. When I'm tall and strong like you, I'm going to marry her!"

We both laughed aloud at the absurdity of his words.

"Oh, I'm sure there is some perfect young lady just for you." She smiled at him.

"Well, I hope so."

"Tristan! Come here, boy! We have to get going." We turned, and the stablemaster was making his way to us, holding the new mare by the reins. She was brown with a white muzzle and a star on her forehead.

"Commander Ronin." The stablemaster nodded to me.

"John."

We said our goodbyes and headed back down the street.

"A wager, huh?"

I stiffened and turned to her to explain. She smiled to my relief as I only saw humor in her eyes when I was sure I would find disappointment or hurt.

"It's not what it seems, and I'd gladly do it all over again," I told her. She flushed at my words and tilted her head down.

"I understand, commander. I'm truly grateful for this new start no matter how it occurred."

Chapter 13

LILLIAN

We made it to the Seamstresses. The shop had lots of windows that displayed the latest fashion of the fae. The front was twice as large as Madam Olgath's shop, and I knew I was in for a treat. As we entered, a bell chimed above us, notifying the shop that someone had arrived.

A robust, tall fae came through with long dark hair pulled half up with a sparkling clip. She was beautiful with her vibrant gray eyes and red lips. A measuring tape wrapped around her neck, and she wore a white apron with scissors poking out and a wristband holding pins. I would know a head seamstress anywhere. This must be Madame Serale.

"Commander, it is so good to see you. I received your note this morning. Then, motioning towards me, "this must be Lillian." She smiled as she walked toward me with open arms, giving me a tight embrace. I already liked her and her welcoming nature. I returned her embrace, and when I stepped back, she picked up my hands and examined them. I became self-conscious and wanted to pull them out of her grasp, but I resisted as she drew them closer to her eyes for inspection and then patted them tenderly.

"Ah, yes. These hands are excellent with a needle. You will do just fine in my shop." Then raising her head, she gave me a knowing smile and continued, "I know talent when I see it, and my dear, you are going to make some beautiful gowns."

I couldn't help the blush that came to my face at her compliment. She patted my hand once more, then released my fingers, which I clasped together in front of me.

"Oh, is this her, Madam Serale?" Came a joyful squeal from the back of the shop. Looking around the head seamstress, I saw a human girl making her way up to the front. She had curly blonde hair, ocean-blue eyes, and a vibrant smile.

"Yes, Chrysta. Come meet our new assistant, Lillian."

She came up and gave me a tight squeeze, just as the seamstress did.

"Thank goodness! You came just in time. We are drowning up to our necks with orders. When my mate told me you were looking for a job here, I about came and got you myself!"

I was confused. I know Ronin said his captain's wife worked here, but she was human like me.

"Chrysta is my captain's wife."

"Oh." I smiled and looked back at the young woman. She only looked a couple of years older than me, and I couldn't recall her living in Retna. Maybe her family came from another town for the festival. I'd ask her about it later once we were more acquainted.

"I'm so glad you need assistance. I was worried I would be barging in."

"Not at all! Right, Madam Serale?"

"Yes, it will be so good to have some extra hands to help around here. I pay a fair wage, and room and board are included."

"Thank you so much. It's more than I hoped for."

"Well, it seems you are taken care of, Lillian. I should be off." Ronin told me as he put my chest down and looked back at me. I was sad to see him leave, not knowing when I would see him again.

I came up to him, and he searched my eyes as if he wanted to say more, but when he didn't, I decided I would.

"Thank you, Ronin, for everything. I hope I will see you around?" I questioned him.

"Of course you will!" Chrysta interrupted, coming up to us.

"I often visit the castle since the commander likes to keep his men, especially *my* mate, from their *poor* wives." She accused him. Then she and Ronin laughed, and I joined in, glad what she said was in jest.

"I can't help that he's one of the few men I trust."

"No doubt!" Then she turned to me. "You can come with me when the shop closes early. It will be nice to have someone to walk with to the castle."

"That would be wonderful."

We said our goodbyes and I watched him leave. My heart sank as the door closed, hoping he'd turn back around with one more glance my way, but I was disappointed as he quickly walked away and out of my sight.

"Don't mind him. He's not one for goodbyes." I turned to see Chrysta looking at me with knowing eyes. No doubt she knew our story, with her mate being the captain and all. Then she smiled, linked my arms with hers, and led me into the backroom where most of our work would be completed.

"Come, let me show you the shop." Then she turned to me with a wide smile. "I think we are going to be the best of friends."

I couldn't help the smile that came to my face, "I think so too!"

After about half an hour of showing me where everything was, I was eager to start. Their material was far superior to anything in Retna. The silk was so smooth and the cotton so thick and sturdy.

Soon, we were settled in comfy chairs and chatting about our lives as we made one stitch after the other.

"So, how long ago were you chosen?" I asked her since she mentioned it while showing me the shop.

"About twenty years ago."

"Twenty? But you look close to my age."

"Oh, that is the wonderful thing about the bond. When humans bond to a fae, they become so interconnected that they share a life force with their mate, and essentially are given immortality."

"Wow, that is amazing," I told her, but I could not help it when blue eyes and a tall broad fae came to my mind, wondering what it would have been like if we had bonded. Putting away such thoughts since they would do me no good, I continued to listen to her story.

"He came to town early. He was eager to choose a bride, but I persuaded him I was the best choice he had." She laughed, and Madam Serale stepped into the room.

"Telling her your story, Chrysta?"

"Only the best love story out there."

"She bribed him with cookies." Madam Serale stated plainly, and I giggled at the absurdity of it.

"It worked for me." She shrugged and smirked, not bothered by Madam Serale's statement. Then turning back to me, "My father was the town baker, and my mother *always* said that the way to a man's heart is through his stomach. I made a batch and had them ready as a thank you for saving me from a hurt ankle." She winked, and I knew she probably planned that too.

Weeks passed, and I soon learned all the different styles the fae wore. They were so different from the town of Retna. Flowy and easier to move in than the layers upon layers we usually sported. I became close with Chrysta like she said we would. She brought a light to my life and filled the void I had from losing Helen and Claira. I often thought about them and hoped they were doing okay.

One morning the doorbell chimed, and heavy footsteps entered instead of the usual chattering and giggles filled with demands for new gowns.

I entered the main room and was surprised to see the captain holding a large chest in his hands. We had previously met on several occasions when Chrysta invited me to walk to the castle with her, not to mention the first night Ronin saved me. I always tried to look for the commander when we walked to the castle grounds, but he was never around.

"Chrysta! Your mate is here." I hollered back to my friend. "Welcome, captain. It's good to see you. Chrysta should be here in a moment."

"I'm actually here to see you." I was surprised when he stepped forward and held out the chest in his hands. "The commander sent me here to give you your dowry."

"Oh." I stepped forward and grabbed it out of his hands, and found it was heavier than I expected, so I put it down at my feet until he left. "Thank you. Did the commander come with you?" I looked around and out the window, hoping he would enter if he had stayed outside.

"No, he was busy with duties, but he also gave me this." He lifted a pocket on his jacket, pulled out a sealed letter, and handed it to me. I took it from his hands and put it in my apron. I would open it later when I was alone.

"Caden!" Chrysta cried as she ran into the room and into his arms. He lifted her up and swung her around, kissing her on the lips. I looked away, not wanting to intrude on their intimate moment together, wishing I had that kind of love in my life. He treated her as if she held the very breath of life in her hands.

I thanked him once more, telling him to let Ronin know I said hi. After he assured me he would, he and Chrysta headed out the door to go home for the day.

I closed shop and lifted the chest to make my way upstairs to the loft that Madam Serale let me stay in. It had two beds, one for me and one for Chrysta, for when Caden was gone with military duties. Putting the chest on the bed, I pulled out the letter from Ronin and used my finger to break the wax seal. A key fell out, and I picked it up off the floor and used it to open the chest. A gasp escaped my lips. The whole chest was filled to the brim with coins. It was a king's bounty, and I would want for nothing with this amount of wealth. Closing the chest and making sure it was locked tightly before placing it under my bed for safekeeping, I quickly went downstairs and grabbed a piece of ribbon from the discard bin where material or ribbon that was too short or had any sort of flaws were placed. I put it through the keyhole and tied it around my neck, placing it under my bodice.

Then, I quickly made my way back upstairs, eager to read the letter Ronin had sent me.

Dear Lillian,

I hope this message finds you well and that you are enjoying the comforts Llor has to offer. Your dowry, paid in full, is in the chest. I hope it will help ease your burdens and bring you the life you deserve.

-Commander Ronin

I couldn't deny I was disappointed by his letter. It was detached, and he didn't even sign it with *your friend or sincerely.* I thought he liked me, even if it was only as a friend, especially with how he initially treated me. He was so caring and protective of me. Now, it was as if I didn't even exist. The letter was impersonal and hollow. I should stop expecting more, though. He told me from the beginning that he was not looking for a bride, but I couldn't let go of this tiny piece of hope that festered inside my chest. Looking to the small hearth in our room, I about tossed the parchment inside to burn and have my thoughts of this man turn to ash with it.

Instead, I folded it up and tucked it away in my drawer. It was time to move on.

Chapter 14

RONIN

I was a coward, and I knew it. I had Lillian's dowry chest for two weeks now, and I made every excuse that I was too busy to deliver it to her; until this morning. Caden said he was going to pick up his wife from the seamstresses and offered for me to tag along. I came up with some lame excuse about making sure the armory was accounted for, but it gave me the opportunity to hand him the chest to deliver along with the most pathetic note.

I was pacing my quarters, thinking over the last month, how I would hide whenever I saw her coming up the road towards the castle with Chrysta to speak with my Captain. One time I hid in the stables, and that led me to an hour-long ride when the stablemaster saddled my horse and handed him to me, thinking I came to do that very thing. I couldn't tell him I was here avoiding a certain girl. While I was honorable, I still had pride. I, the commander of the army of Llor, would rather fight a shadowland Orta than face this beauty, who was the very opposite of frightening. While Ortas had large fangs and dangly appendages, hid deep within the shadowland swamps and were rarely seen. This girl who haunted my thoughts was quick to smile and had a calm and quiet manner that drew me to her. Yes, while she was not as frightening, she was definitely more dangerous than any shadowland monster.

Needing to get my head clear, I decided to visit Leon and discuss the reports on the ogres latest endeavors. As of late, they have been getting more risky and open with their raids. A town on the far side of Llor lost some houses, and many were injured. I needed to gather some of my men and put an end to this. It would also get me away from Llor for a while and a certain seamstress who wouldn't leave my thoughts.

I headed towards the King's study and walked right in.

"Ronin. Just the man I need to see." He turned and smiled at me from his desk.

"Come sit. I have some news." He told me, pointing to the oversized chair in front of his desk. I walked over quickly and sat down.

"Is it about the ogres?"

"Not exactly, but we do need to discuss that too."

"Good. That's why I'm here."

"Perfect, but first, I wanted to tell you I decided to hold a ball."

I thought of any special occasions coming up, but the fall festival was still a few months away.

"What's the occasion, your majesty?"

"Oh, simply for the people. I need to speak with some Lords about the raids, how they are holding up, and what we can do better to keep their lands safe and secure." I nodded in agreement as he continued. "We'll open the gates, and it will be a perfect opportunity for everyone."

Then he looked me up and down with a glint in his eye. "Also, you'll need new attire."

I was confused. "I just got my new uniform recently."

"Nope." He cut me off. "I have a specific design in mind." Then he smiled to himself. "Yes, this will be perfect. I'll call the seamstress and have her come over immediately to have you and your men measured and fitted. She'll probably need all of her assistants, too."

I finally knew what game he was playing at.

"This is nonsense. I don't need a new uniform. I've barely worn the ones we have." I did all I could to avoid a certain assistant from Madam Serale's shop, and he was ruining it for me.

"That's why I'm having a ball." He answered as if it was obvious. It wasn't. It wasted time and resources when he could just send letters to the Lords who had jurisdiction in other cities and towns of Llor and figure it out from there.

"Oh, and you have to bring someone with you."

He thought he was sly, but I would win this round.

"I can't, Your Majesty, I have my work cut out for me, and that has never been a requirement for any event you have held so far."

Didn't I come here to tell him it would be wise to send another scouting group out to check the ogres, not to plan a ball?

I hated balls.

"It has. It's just *you* refuse to bring anyone. Plus, you can't do anything until I have more information from the Lords and their lands anyway, Ronin."

He was right, as much as I didn't like it.

Then he looked down and to the side, not keeping eye contact with me as his gaze roamed the room. "Oh, and since a certain seamstress will be coming, maybe you could ask her to go with you?"

I knew it.

I scoffed at his insufferable matchmaking. "Fine. I'll bring someone." I told him to quiet him up, but I was not going to say who. Grateful he seemed satisfied with my answer since he did not bring it up again. We continued to discuss plans for helping our kingdom and not about the newest assistant to the seamstress.

❦

A week later, I was out with some of my men scouting the edges of our borders. Relieved Leon agreed to it when we had our discussion previously and when one of my scouts returned saying the ogres were going to hold a meeting in a week; I prepared my men.

It was dark, and we were hiding behind trees with a spell that helped us blend in with our surroundings. Thanking fate that the moon was hidden behind the clouds, which only helped keep our cover from our rivals. My most skilled archers had their bows out and ready, awaiting my signal. The rest of me and I had our swords drawn, prepared for anything that may happen or come our way since we were so close to the ogre's cave, only a hundred paces away. I didn't want to take any chances, even though we were just here to observe. The reason was that a certain dark fae prince was speaking with its leader yet again, and I would hate to be caught off guard. They sat around a large fire discussing their latest endeavors. The prince had his men around him, but I knew there were some hidden from our eyes.

Fae had excellent hearing, so I was able to catch part of their conversation.

"We need to continue our training, but it will have to be on my brother's lands." Prince Devron told Dret, the ogre leader.

"Why not training be here? We capable doing as prince order. Ogres fierce and listen to Dret." The large leader demanded as he pounded his chest with a fist, towering over the prince.

I almost regretted not interfering those months ago when his highness was at the festival, but it was too late now. I looked around, wondering where his commander was, then back to the prince, who quickly looked towards the woods where we were hiding. I held my breath and kept still, knowing he would catch any movement.

"You think ogres dumb, incapable of orders, Dret prove prince wrong."

"No! You must stay low and wait for my command. We have an alliance, and you agreed to its terms."

"Dret take no orders from prince!" He lifted his fist to hit the young fae, but the prince was quick, and the ogre was flat on his face with a swish of the prince's hand in a blink of an eye, as his power wrapped around the ogre leader.

"You will do as I say, or there will be consequences." He hissed at the large ogre, now struggling on the dirt against the power that held him captive.

The ogre nodded the best he could, and the prince released him. He faltered as he stood, then crossed his arms and glared at Devron.

"We will train again soon. Get your men ready, we don't have time to delay, and I will expect complete compliance from your men next time. Understood?"

The ogre grunted, and the prince whipped around, opened a portal, and was gone. No doubt going back to his dark lair and cruel brother who ruled their lands. We stayed to observe until all the ogres were inside their cave. I mulled over what I heard. It seemed King Kadrell of the dark fae lands was planning something big, and he was using his brother to gather allies to help execute them. While I was almost positive it was towards our lands, I still needed more information on their timeline. I signaled to my men that we were done observing, and we opened our own portals to head back to Llor. I needed to prepare my men and let the king know what we found out since dark plans were being formed against our kingdom.

Chapter 15

RONIN

"Oh, and before I forget, the seamstresses will be here soon. I need you to gather your men in the great hall for measurements."

I barely finished discussing what we learned from my excursion and was taken off guard when he mentioned that a certain girl would be at the castle within the hour.

"I don't need a new uniform, Leon." Trying my best to get out of being in any proximity to that woman.

"Nonsense! I won't hear any more about it, Ronin. Go get your men and gather in the hall."

"Yes, Your Majesty." Trying to keep the sense of defeat out of my voice. There was only so much you could do when your closest friend was also the King of your land.

I quickly gathered my men and headed to the great hall, surprised to see the seamstresses were already there waiting for us, but only one captured my attention. I could not seem to take my eyes off her as I ordered my men to line up for their measurements.

She glanced at me and gave me a small smile. My heart started pounding in my chest, grateful she turned to begin measuring my men before I did something foolish. I kept glancing at her as she moved down the line, measuring each of my soldiers. I told myself I was just observing her work as she asked my men's names, telling them to lift their arms and turn so she could wrap the tape around them. I had to tamper down my emotions when she touched them, wanting to remove her hands from them. They didn't deserve her touch. I had to keep reminding myself she was just doing her job to measure them for new uniforms. Then I realized she would be doing the same thing to me soon, and I panicked, but the more I observed her, the more I noticed something different about her.

This girl was not the same timid young woman I took away from that wretched town of Retna so long ago.

My thoughts were interrupted by the glorious sound that escaped her mouth. She was laughing at something one of my men said. Envy swept through me that I wasn't the one who caused her to feel that emotion and create that beautiful sound that echoed throughout the great hall. I turned away from her and looked at my Captain, who was now being measured by his wife. He leaned down and whispered something in her ear and she nodded at his words. The only place I could look was up, to give them the privacy they needed.

It also meant that I was next, and I realized I might lose the chance of having Lillian close to me since she was still about five soldiers away from me.

I was surprised when Chrysta walked right by me when she was done measuring her husband and went on to the next soldier. She looked at Lillian, then back to me, and winked.

"Lillian, the commander still needs to be measured. Could you please do that while I finish up with the rest?" She called to her friend.

I froze, and panic again coursed through me at her intervention. I was a mess of emotions, and I hated myself for it.

"Of course." She replied and headed my way. What was wrong with me? A few moments ago, I couldn't wait to have her hands on my chest measuring me, and now I was as jumpy as a young foal. I looked to my captain for help and maybe a way to escape, but he only had a broad smile and a twinkle in his eye. I knew he told his wife to skip me and give me to Lillian.

I gulped as the girl I've been trying to avoid so far, yet anticipated her nearness, stepped in front of me. It was too late now.

"Hello, Commander. It's been a long time." She softly told me with a voice that made my heart pound out of my chest, knowing I would give myself away when she measured me.

"Two months exactly," I spilled out quickly before I could stop myself, not believing I just told her that. I sounded like a smitten fool who had desperately been waiting for his lover to return, and I mentally kicked myself for it. I also hated the formality between us. I wanted to hear my name on her lips again but thought better of it since my men surrounded me, and I didn't want them to think anything was between this girl and me.

I had an army to run, not a courtship to pursue.

"Yes, two months." She sounded unhappy, and I became worried.

"Has Llor not been to your liking?"

She quickly smiled at me, "oh, it has been such a dream. Thank you again for all you have done for me."

I wish I could have done more. I would give her the world if I could.

"I'm so glad to hear that." I told her instead of revealing my true thoughts.

She gently put her hands under my arms and raised them herself instead of telling me to lift them to the side like I watched her do for the others. She took a couple of measurements, then, to my surprise, wrapped her arms around my waist instead of walking around as she did to my men. I had the urge to keep her there and stopped myself from wrapping my own arms around her and pulling her closer. Her head pressed against my chest as she reached around to grab the other side of the measuring tape. No doubt in my mind that she could hear the pounding of my heart due to her close proximity.

She stepped back, and I immediately missed her warmth. She brought the tape measure closer to her eyes, took the pad out from her white apron, and wrote the measurements down with a pencil she took from behind her ear. She put the pad back in her apron and brought the measuring tape up to my chest. Her fingers moved to line up the measurements correctly. Bringing a tingling sensation wherever she touched me. I was utterly captivated by her.

My captain cleared his throat, and I looked over to see him smirking at me.

I returned it with a glare, and he muffled a laugh with his fists as he turned the other way.

"Are you going to the ball, commander?"

Chapter 16

LILLIAN

I realized he was glaring at his captain when I asked him the question that was burning on my tongue. I should have waited or probably not asked at all. We received an invitation earlier this week, along with the request to provide his men with some new uniforms. The days dragged on until I finally stepped into the great hall to see his tall, masculine figure calling me out. I told myself I wouldn't react when I saw him since I had moved on and did great until I noticed he was the next man to be measured by Chrysta. I realized I should have taken the opportunity to measure him first, since he *was* the commander, instead of starting at the end of the line. Grateful my friend let me have the honor since she knew what he had done for me and my situation. At least, that is what I told myself. I hoped my infatuation for him wasn't that obvious.

He turned wide-eyed to me when I asked him about attending the ball. He stared at me for a few moments without responding. I flushed, realizing I should have bit my tongue. He probably thought I was forward and wanted him to ask me. While it was true, I did not want him to believe me desperate. He has already done so much for me.

Realizing I wasn't going to get an answer after a few moments of him staring at me with shock, I pushed my disappointment down and continued to measure him as if nothing had changed.

"Yes." He stated slowly, and I waited, anticipating more, but moments passed without another word, and I knew he was not going to say anymore. Nodding my head, I turned to move on to the next man in line when suddenly he grabbed my hand.

"Are you?" he asked desperately, but maybe that was my imagination filling in the disappointment that perhaps he would ask me after all.

"Attending the ball?" wanting to make certain that is what he was asking.

He nodded.

Feeling bold, I gazed into his mesmerizing eyes that always pulled me in before I could stop myself and said, "Only if someone asks me."

It seemed an eternity went by as we looked into each other's eyes while I anticipated his response.

Then he broke the connection and looked off into the distance.

"Maybe I'll see you there then." he curtly told me with no emotion.

Understanding his meaning left a gaping hole in my heart. I nodded and forced the tears back at his rejection. Turning to the next fae, I continued down the line, measuring each of his soldiers the same as I did before, only quicker. I couldn't wait to escape this hall and his overwhelming presence. There were only a few left to measure, to my relief, and soon I would be done and away from the place.

"Name?" I asked the soldier next in line for measurements.

"Drew."

I wrote his name on a separate page where I would put his personal measurements, as I did for the other men before me.

"Please hold your arms out to the side."

He did as I asked, and I took the measuring tape from around my neck, glancing at Ronin as I did. His face was still turned away from me, not giving away any emotion.

Where was the kind man who rescued me? Maybe it was good I didn't marry him if this was how he would have treated me the rest of our days. His kindness was replaced with indifference, and I deserved so much more than that. Being in Llor and surrounded by people who cared helped show me my worth, and I wouldn't waste it on those who didn't see that. Even as I tried to convince myself that I deserved so much more, my heart still ached at his treatment of me.

I went through the motions of measuring the soldier's chest, arms, and wrists. When I brought the measuring tape around to wrap it around his neck, he grabbed my hands. I pulled back, shocked at his forwardness even though previously I welcomed the commander's.

"Sorry, my lady, I didn't mean to frighten you, but I don't think you heard my question," he said gently with a small smile.

"Oh, I'm sorry. I was focusing on measuring you. Please, do ask again." That is when I noticed the soldier before me for the first time. He was tall and had short blond hair and blue eyes, but not as blue as someone else's. I shook my thoughts. He didn't want me. He's made it clear on multiple occasions, from weeks ago and within the last five minutes. Why did my resolve to move on from this man crumble the moment I saw him, even though he treated me with indifference?

"I was asking if you were going to the ball?"

Did he hear my conversation with Ronin? My answer changed since then, I would rather stay home than see him dance with all the beautiful fae women that were constantly entering my shop. I was nothing compared to them. Maybe that was part of the reason he kept avoiding me. I was human and nothing compared to the fae who lived in Llor, at least in his eyes. I was treated with respect and equally in the town just outside the castle gates.

"I'm not sure." I told him slowly and hesitantly.

"It would be my honor if I could escort you."

I couldn't help but steal a glance at the man who made me doubt my worth to see him watching me with folded arms and a firm mouth.

I turned back to the soldier before me, who watched me with eagerness, anticipating my answer, obviously not seeing his commander's reaction.

I barely turned my head, not wanting to be caught looking at him again, only to see Ronin now glaring at me with fury in his eyes, and I couldn't help but shrink back. Suddenly, he whipped around and stomped towards the doors of the great hall. Anger rose in me at his behavior. I was done pining for this man who was now acting like a child. While I was grateful for all he did to set me on my feet, but he had no say in what I did or didn't do with my life, and it seemed even friendship between us was out of reach. I would put him out of my mind once and for all. He didn't deserve my attention, thoughts, or anything else from me, not if he was going to treat me like this. I've already suffered years from that at the hands of my father and others who lived in Retna. Not anymore.

I turned back to the handsome soldier before me to reply to his question.

"The honor would be mine." I gave him my most charming smile, to which he returned, but if I was honest, my heart was breaking.

Chapter 17

RONIN

I brought my sword back around and hit the thick post that was used for practice, making deep dents in the wood with my powerful blows. Wood chips flew everywhere around me. If I kept this up we'd no longer have a post, but new kindling to be used this winter for starting the castle's fires.

"I knew I'd find you here." I turned and saw my captain leaning against another post of the practice yard. All the humor from earlier was gone and replaced with a look of reprimand.

"What happened back there?" He pointed to the castle.

"I don't know what you are talking about?"

"You can't fool me, Ronin. I know you care for the girl, but to treat her with such disdain, to which I may note, she did *not* deserve."

The guilt I already felt for being rude to her grew at his words, and I tried to push them down to no avail. "I've done my duty. There is nothing to talk about."

"Duty?" he scoffed as he pushed off the post and walked towards me. I dropped my sword to my side, my breaths coming out heavily from my exercise.

"There is more to life than duty and honor, Ronin."

"Like what?"

"Love."

It was my turn to scoff. "I don't have time for love. I have a Kingdom to protect and duties to fulfill to ensure that. You, of all people, should know the great responsibility that rests on our shoulders."

He shook his head at my words, and my frustration flared once again.

"Enough, Captain. Know your place, and don't speak of it again," I ordered him.

He looked at me with pity in his eyes as he nodded to heed my command. I turned to leave, but he called out to me, and I stopped but didn't turn back to face him.

"I hope you find what you're looking for, Ronin, because the greatest things in life will never be reached in this training yard, with your men, or any heroic mission you accomplish, but only with those we love."

I thought about the truth of his words for a moment and turned to respond, only to find he was no longer there. I sighed and returned to my quarters, trying to convince myself he was wrong. I didn't need anyone in my life. I reached fulfillment in my duties, with my men and protecting my kingdom, but I couldn't help the sinking feeling in my chest that I was somehow wrong and maybe the captain was right.

Chapter 18

LILLIAN

"Oh, you look fabulous!" Chrysta told me as she placed her hands over her mouth in awe. I came down the stairs from my loft in a new dress I'd been working on for weeks in my spare time for the upcoming ball. It was the color of sapphire and shined when the light hit it. I twirled it around when I reached the bottom of the stairs. It formed to my body and flared at the bottom. My long sleeves were tight until about a quarter of the way down, where they opened up to reveal my forearms. Around my neck was a simple pendant with a simmering oval in the middle, made of crystal and surrounded by an intricate silver design that kept the gem in place.

"Thank you, Chrysta. You look beautiful as well."

"It helps when you work at the best seamstress shop in all the fae lands." She smiled at me. We've become so close the last few months, and I know I would be lost and lonely without her friendship in these fae lands.

She twirled as well so I could admire the final product she worked tirelessly to create. The gown was fuchsia, and similar to the style I was wearing. We decided to work on our dresses together after the shop closed in the evening. Then tonight we decided to help each other get ready for the ball. The captain would pick us up along with the soldier who asked me to attend the ball with him.

A knock came on the door, and she made her way over to answer. I looked myself over again in the mirror before we headed out. My hair was done up in a twisted style that Chrysta helped me with. My friend wore her hair down and curled to perfection. She really would outshine everyone at the ball.

I turned when footsteps came into our shop. Chrysta was hanging onto her mate's arm, and he was looking at her with such love in his eyes. I turned to Drew, not wanting to be caught staring at their intimate moment.

He looked handsome in his formal military attire. We were still working on their new uniforms, so I assumed these were the old ones. They looked in excellent condition, and I wondered why they needed to be replaced. I would not complain too much, though, it brought in a hefty sum for the shop, and we were able to buy more materials for our customers to choose from. Along with a bonus in our pay. The uniforms they came to pick us up in were black with silver round buttons up the front and light gray tassels at the shoulders. They had a short stiff collar and some sort of symbol that either represented rank or occupation. The Kingdom of Llor's symbol was over their right chest; a white rose in front of crossing swords and a crown. The cut was exquisite, and I didn't doubt that Madam Serale was the one who stitched this soldier's uniform. She was an enchantress with a needle and thread.

After looking over his uniform, I realized he had a broad smile and was looking at me with a gleam in his eyes. I blushed, realizing he caught me gawking at him. It wasn't my fault my occupation made me notice every new piece of clothing that I came across. He stepped forward to give me a short bow.

"Lady Lillian, you look absolutely stunning. I feel honored to escort you tonight."

"Thank you, Drew. You look wonderful as well."

He held out his arm to me and led me out the door. I was surprised to see a carriage out front being pulled by two large black horses.

I turned to Chrysta for answers. I was under the impression we would be walking to the castle since it was such a short distance.

"Privileges of being the captain." Her husband told me. I smiled at his reply. Grateful our dresses would now stay dust-free from the dirt roads. I knew Chrysta and Drew had their own beautiful cottage at the edge of town. I visited often when she would invite me for supper but didn't realize how expansive that wealth was.

We got to the carriage door, and I turned to see Drew holding his hand out for me to take.

"May I?"

"Yes. Thank you."

He took my hand and helped me into the large carriage that was covered in plush seating.

I made my way over to the edge of the seat and sat down, making space for my escort. Once everyone was settled, the captain tapped the roof and called out to the driver that we were ready. The carriage jolted forward, and everyone chuckled as we moved with the carriage and started our journey towards the castle.

"I hear everyone in the village was invited, and it should be a grand event," Caden spoke to our small party.

"I can't wait to dance and see all the dresses Lillian and I worked so hard to finish this last month. My fingers can finally rest. I've never sewn so many gowns in such a short amount of time." Chrysta said looking at her fingers.

She was right. I looked down at my own fingers, which had an imprint from the needle constantly in our hand. We had to work extra hours to fulfill all our orders to make sure they were ready in time for the ball, along with the large order of new uniforms for the king's army. Grateful we had more time to fulfill that order since the king said he wasn't in a rush.

"I agree. It will be nice to finally give my fingers a break."

"Did you make the gowns you are wearing?" Drew inquired.

"Yes, we did," I told him.

"You have a remarkable talent, and I can't wait to see the others in the gowns you have made." Then he looked straight into my eyes, "but none will outshine yours or your beauty."

I blushed at his compliment. "Thank you."

I thought over the last few weeks of getting to know this soldier. He always greeted me when I came with Chrysta to see the captain, and have gotten to know him better through our small conversations. Last week when I finished delivering a gown to a customer, I returned to the shop to see a large vase full of flowers he had delivered just for me. It was my birthday, but I didn't recall telling him since I didn't want a big fuss to be made about it. Chrysta let it slip that she may have told him when she brought out a sweet cake she baked for me. I felt so loved and was more grateful than ever to be here in Llor.

I looked up at this man who was always a gentleman and treated me respectfully. I didn't have strong feelings towards him, only that of friendship, but it was a start towards realizing that I had a place in Llor and not just among my friends at the shop. That maybe I could dream of having a family one day, and it filled me with joy.

Soon, the carriage stopped, and the men exited first so they could help us down the small steps.

Drew held his arm out to me and I wrapped my fingers around the crook of his arm as he led me to the ballroom. Thoughts of the commander were far from my mind as I anticipated a lovely evening with friends and dancing.

Chapter 19

RONIN

I noticed her the moment she entered the ballroom. She was gorgeous in her sapphire dress, the only thing I hated was that she was hanging onto one of my men, who had no right to escort her to the ball.

No, he had every right, I quickly reprimanded myself. It was I who didn't. I knew Drew was a good man and a great soldier. I couldn't fault him for taking an interest in Lillian when her kind, sweet, and caring nature, not to mention her beauty, would make any man or fae want to be in her presence.

"Everything okay, Commander?" I turned to Lady Eliza, the daughter of Fae Lord Duren. She had a worried look on her pale face that matched her pale eyes. Nothing compared to the striking brown eyes that barely entered the room. I was her escort for the evening. While she was good company and we talked about a few things happening in our kingdom, I really wanted to be somewhere else.

"Yes, everything is fine. Thank you." I turned quickly from the beauty who was now dancing and laughing in the arms of her escort.

"I wondered what your opinion was on the raids?" She asked me, but I was no longer surprised by her questions. Her father had jurisdiction over the town of Treamon, and they recently had a skirmish with the ogres.

"What have you been doing to prevent them?" she asked with an accusatory tone. I stiffened and held back my reply. This girl knew nothing about the sacrifice me and my men made every day for this kingdom. Early this week, we gathered most of my men to ambush the ogre's cave to finish them once and for all. This war went on long enough, but when we arrived, they were nowhere to be found. When all of a sudden, they jumped out of nowhere. It was as if they had a cloaking spell on them, but I didn't know how since they had no magic in their blood. I noticed the ogres were glowing with some blue force that enhanced their strength and stamina since we ended up fighting for our lives, and I knew immediately that the dark fae prince had a hand in their unusual power. We were able to escape with no deadly injuries, to my great relief. My men were like family, and any loss hit close to my heart.

I placed a hand on my ribs, which were still healing from the event. Grateful for my fae healing powers that allowed me to be here tonight.

"Well, commander?"

I put on as much charm as I could muster before responding. This woman knew nothing about sacrifice.

"My men and I are doing everything we can to prevent any more raids. I'm sorry about Treamon."

She huffed at me and looked away towards those currently dancing. I was about to leave the ballroom, and her standing there. I was tired, irritated, and angry at myself, and I didn't need some Lord's daughter making it worse.

"Would you like a drink?" I asked her. It was more of an excuse to get away from her for a few minutes than to be a good escort.

"Yes, thank you."

I quickly made my escape, wondering how long I could stand by the refreshments without being rude. I made my way over, got a clean glass, and filled it with a fruity punch famous in the fae lands.

"Commander! It is so good to see you here."

I turned to see my captain with his wife at his side, looking at me with smiles on their faces. I glanced around them to see if a certain young woman was with them.

"She's over there." My commander laughed as he pointed to Lillian, who was still dancing and smiling brightly at her partner.

I decided to play ignorance. "Who?"

Then he stepped closer while rolling his eyes and whispered. "I'm sure she wouldn't mind if you cut it."

I sighed and looked at the two glasses in my hand that were filled with punch, then back to Lady Eliza.

"I can deliver those." My captain missed nothing as he gazed to where Lady Eliza was standing, waiting for me. "I know Lady Eliza, so an introduction wouldn't need to be made."

"I couldn't possibly…" Then he snatched the drinks from my hand and nodded towards the dance floor. I gave him a small smile.

"You can thank me later, commander. Maybe a day off so my wife knows I'm married to her and not the King's army?"

I chuckled, knowing he said it in good humor, but I may just fulfill his desire since he gave me a break from Lady Eliza.

Then he left me and I watched as they went over to the girl I was *supposed* to be dancing with. Chrysta immediately started a conversation about Lady Eliza's gown, and she responded with eagerness. Knowing she would be okay for a few minutes, I made my way onto the dance floor, hoping the partner I was about to steal would be just as eager to be in my arms as much as I wanted her there.

Chapter 20

LILLIAN

"Oh, Drew, I'm having such a great time!" I told the fae who had been twirling me around the dance floor since we entered the ballroom. I couldn't help the smile and laughter that kept escaping my lips.

"I'm so glad." He pulled me closer and spun me around again, my stomach fluttering at our closeness.

"Ah-hem." We both stopped and turned towards our interruption. My stomach instantly felt queasy, but my traitorous heart fluttered as piercing blue eyes stared straight into mine. He was wearing the same attire as the other men in his regime. Only a few more symbols and badges were placed on the front, along with silver stripes down the sides of his arms, no doubt showing his rank.

He broke our connection and turned to Drew, who was now stiff and standing at attention, waiting for his commander's orders.

"May I?" Ronin asked him, motioning towards me, and panic swept over me. I didn't know if I was more scared or eager to be in his arms. No, what was I thinking, I didn't want this man who rejected me over and over again anywhere near me, and I had to tamper any anger that grew at his impertinence to cut in and ask for my hand to dance after he avoided me for months.

I knew he came with someone else, so why wasn't he dancing with her instead? Not that I was looking for him when I entered the ballroom, he's just hard to miss with his overbearing presence. That's at least what I told myself when I spotted him with a beautiful fae in this large room full of people on the opposite side of the expansive room.

"Of course, Commander." Drew told him with a quick bow. Then he glanced at me and smiled, "You're in good hands, Lady Lillian." Then he handed me off to the commander and left quickly. I almost felt abandoned and looked around to see where he was going. Didn't he know I didn't want to dance with his commander? Of course not, but I was at least grateful when he made his way over to Caden, and Chrysta, who was still speaking with the girl Ronin brought to the event.

"Don't worry. You'll be back in his arms before you know it." He said with boredom, but his eyes gave away a different emotion.

I nodded. Any words I did have stuck in my throat.

He pulled me onto the dance floor, and I realized a waltz was now starting to my demise. I placed my hand in his and a tingle shot up my arm. His other hand reached around my waist and pulled me closer than was necessary. My heart beating out of my chest at our proximity.

"You look beautiful, Lillian." He told me softly. My suppressed anger rushed to the surface at his words. I was tired of his games and at myself for reacting to him. First, he saves me, treating me as if I mattered to him. Then, he treats me with disdain and glares at me, only to call me beautiful?

"I don't understand, commander." I tried to keep the venom out of my voice, but it slipped through.

"Don't understand?" his eyebrows pulling together in confusion. I stopped our dancing and pulled him to the side, behind a large pillar that would hide both of us, not caring about decorum or decency. I had words for him, and I didn't need an audience.

"What do you want from me? You treat me as if you care and are glad to save me from my miserable life in Retna, only to shun me as if I have the plague. Then you dare to intrude on me again to show you have authority over a soldier who has only treated me kindly." I hissed at him.

"I...I'm not..."

"I'm grateful for all you have done for me, but if you don't want me in your life..." I gulped as I realized tears were now streaming down my face. I went to wipe them away, mad at myself for crying over this fae, but he gently pushed my hands back down and cupped both sides of my cheeks to wipe them away with his thumbs. I had to push down any emotions he was making me feel, holding on to the anger as if my life depended on it, but it was slipping away faster than I wanted.

"Lillian, it's not that I..." he paused

"Not what, commander? I know you say you don't have time for a wife, but could we at least be friends?" I asked, desperately needing to know his answer. I couldn't move on, not if he kept interacting with me like this. It wasn't fair to my heart.

He looked around the ballroom and back to me, his eyes searching mine. I knew I could love this man so easily if he would only let me, but if that is not what he wanted, I needed to know so I could move on.

"No. I can't…" I didn't let him finish as I turned and fled the room, my heart breaking as tears streamed down my cheeks. I wish I never came to this place. Nothing hurts worse than a broken heart.

Chapter 21

RONIN

She fled before I could finish. Looking around to where Lady Eliza was, I was grateful she was still occupied and now laughing with Drew.

Good, that would give me time.

I stepped from behind the pillar to chase after the girl who stole my heart, only to be confronted by my captain. I looked and saw his wife rushing after Lillian.

"What happened, Ronin?" Caden looked at me, then back to his wife, who was now exiting the doors to follow her friend.

"Just a misunderstanding." I went to push past my captain to follow her only to have him place a hand on my arm, stopping me from chasing her..

"Let Chrysta talk with her first to calm her down. She's been through a lot in a short amount of time." Then paused and pursed his lips, "It's hard loving a fae. Especially one as stubborn and prideful as you."

No. She didn't love me. How could she when I gave her no chance to do such a thing. I turned to my captain with raised brows.

"She doesn't love me," I told him plainly.

"Then you are blind." He sighed, "wait until she comes back, and you'll see."

Then he wrapped an arm around my shoulders and led me to the opposite side of the ballroom where Leon was conversing with many noblemen who were attending tonight. No doubt he was discussing solutions for the ogre raids. He looked at us as we approached and excused himself, making his way towards us. We bowed and exchanged formal greetings that were due.

"So, where is Lady Lillian?" Leon said as he scanned the room, excitement in his eyes.

"She's with my wife freshening up." The captain told his majesty, saving me from having to explain how I failed yet again to keep the girl in my good graces.

"Well, I would like to dance with her when she returns."

A growl escaped my throat, and he just laughed.

"Oh, Ronin, if I knew it would be this much fun to match you up with a girl from Retna, I would have done it a long time ago."

"There was no match, only a lost wager." I reminded him. "Which is why I will never let it happen again." It caused me too much chaos in my life, and it was all because of him.

"We'll see." He told me with a grin, "There is time for such talk later though. How are you enjoying the ball so far?"

We talked for a few minutes about the event before it turned to the ogre raids that had been occurring.

"I think our only solution would be to build a wall around our borders. Some of the Lords do not agree on such a thing. They are afraid that if we close our borders, it would ruin any other chances for open trade, but they don't understand it would only provide safety, not diminish our trade routes."

I agreed with him, but could not reply since one of my men came rushing up to us, grabbing our attention. He wasn't in his formal attire, but a scouting uniform. A sinking feeling filled me that something was wrong. Very wrong indeed.

"Your Majesty, commander! Ogres are outside the gates. They appeared out of nowhere and have captured one of our own."

"Caden! Caden!" We turned to see Chrysta running towards us. Her hair was a mess with scrapes on her face and arms. I looked, hoping Lillian was following right behind her, but I knew I wouldn't find her.

"It's Lillian! They took Lillian!"

Everything became a blur as I rushed past everyone in the ballroom, making my way out to the courtyard. My only thoughts were about saving the girl. My heart pounded, not from running, but from the fear that took over me that I would never see her beautiful brown eyes looking up at me again, and the smile that melted any resolve I had to never take a mate. It was then I realized what a fool I had been. I let my pride, not honor, keep me from living life to the fullest. I hoped I wasn't too late in realizing I may have made the biggest mistake of my life.

Once I reached the courtyard full of those on duty, waiting for my orders on how to proceed, an officer rushed up to me.

"Commander, what do we do? They came out of nowhere. Some of us tried to stop them, but their strength was beyond what we could fight off. They took one of our own. How are we to proceed?"

I forced myself to take a breath and not charge after her. I needed all the information I could before I lost all rationality. "Where did they head out?"

He told me how they came, their bodies glowing with some magic that almost cost us our lives last week. The dark prince just gained a formidable enemy because of it. Never again would I allow him to hurt those I love.

"Then they opened a portal and were gone."

"Thank you, Officer Kent. Tell your men to stay alert. I want all posts to have extra men on guard and to alert me of any changes. I am going to gather a small rescue party and go after the girl."

He saluted and left to fulfill my orders.

"I'm coming."

"Me too."

I turned and saw my most trusted friends walking toward me.

"No. You must stay here. I can't lose anyone else I care about tonight."

"We can't lose you either, Commander." Caden stepped up to me and put one of his hands on my right shoulder and Leon came up and did the same on my left.

"Sometimes, the most honorable thing you can do is rely on those you trust." Leon told me.

"When did you become so wise, Your Majesty?" I smirked at him, trying to hide how his words affected me.

"I've always been wise. You're just too stubborn to notice." He smiled in return.

"Okay, let us make a plan." Caden interrupted. I was grateful for both of these men as we quickly formed a plan on how to rescue Lillian. Soon, we were opening a portal and stepping through to the edge of our lands. An ogre's cave shone just ahead.

Chapter 22

LILLIAN

"Let me go!" I pounded against the large ogre's back for the millionth time that night. It couldn't end like this, not when I finally had a life that I enjoyed, even if a particular commander wasn't in it. I had friends, work, and a sense of worth that I never had in Retna. I wouldn't let this ugly brute with tusks take that away from me.

"No! Dret prove to prince he strong and capable."

"You ugly brute! Let me down!"

"Quiet! Hurt Dret ears with screeching!"

I only screamed louder, and he dropped me high off the ground. I landed on my backside, and pain shot through my hip and down my leg. I worried I broke something and tried to move my hip only to cry out as pulsing pain shot down my leg again. How could I ever escape now? I looked around, and it seemed we were in front of a cave entrance that was part of a large rocky terrain. The only way I could tell was because the moon was full, and its beams shone down on it.

Thoughts swirled through my head. I should have never left the ballroom, but at least Chrysta was safe. When she followed me out into the hall after Ronin rejected me once again, I told her I wanted to go home. We started to walk down the path outside the castle gates, only to be jumped by ogres. They took Chrysta first, but I grabbed a large branch and started to hit the brute. He dropped her and reached for me. The next thing I knew, here I was.

"Prince! Prince! Dret and ogres capable!" He hollered to the mouth of the cave.

Prince? Who was he talking to? I turned towards the cave entrance, which started to glow orange with light. A tall, dark-haired fae exited with a larger fae behind him, holding a torch that provided the light. He turned to me, and his eyes went wide with horror. I noticed he looked tired as if his body was drained of energy. He pinched his nose and looked at the ogre named Dret.

"What were you thinking? That was not part of the exercise." He reprimanded the giant ogre, who was twice his height and muscle. I was almost scared for him.

"You say ogres not stealthy. Dret prove to prince." He pointed at me.

"No! You just created a problem!" He shouted back, and I noticed the same power that was surrounding the ogre earlier when he captured me was now pulsing out of his hands. The large burly fae next to him put a hand on his shoulder, and it seemed to calm the prince down. Then the large man nodded towards me, and the prince headed my way. I tried to move, but I couldn't. I prayed he would have compassion on me and set me free.

He bent down in front of me and looked over my body, his eyebrows drawing together.

"You're hurt. Here, let me help you."

"Touch her, and you die at this very moment."

We both turned to see Ronin coming out of the darkness with his sword pointed at the prince. I've never seen him so livid before, and if it weren't for the hope that soared through me that he came, I would have been scared for my own life.

"Step away from her now." He gritted through clenched teeth as he made his way towards us. The prince sighed and stood up to face the commander.

"This is a misunderstanding." He said while putting his hands up as if to surrender and ease the situation.

"Tell that to my men who suffered from last week's battle. I highly doubt your words, Your Majesty." He seethed as he leaped in front of me and brought his sword down on the prince in a deadly blow, but the prince's body blocked it with some magical force that pushed Ronin back and to the side.

The prince's hands and forearms were pulsing with power now, and Ronin pushed his own magic into his sword. I noticed its color for the first time. It glowed white and pure, just as he was. They stared at each other, waiting to see who would make the next move.

"Commander!" I turned to see the large fae rushing up to them. "It's a misunderstanding. His Highness didn't mean for this to happen."

"Lies!" Then he turned back to the prince. "I should have finished you off at the festival when I had the chance!" he growled as he struck the prince, who used the time Ronin was distracted to unsheathe his own sword. They went back and forth, striking and jabbing at one another. Their power whipping around each other, adding strength to their blows. I prayed we would make it out alive and that nothing would happen to the man who came to rescue me.

They fought with skill and precision, and I watched with my heart pounding every time the prince got the upper hand. After a few heart-wrenching moments, Ronin finally hooked the prince's sword and flung it out of his hands, making it land far away from him. They were both breathing hard from their fight, and the prince raised his hands in defeat, standing straight with pride.

"Do it, commander." The prince hissed at him in a challenge.

I held my breath, waiting to see what he would do. He started to raise his sword but I had to stop him before he did something he regretted.

"Ronin! Stop!" I begged him. "Don't do it." I could tell he was listening even though he moved his sword to the prince's neck.

"I got hurt, but before you arrived, the prince was going to help me. Please, spare him…for me." He didn't move but continued to glare at the prince. Then finally, after what seemed like an eternity, he slowly lowered his sword.

"It seems fate is on your side, but let it be known that if I ever see your worthless face again or you harm anyone I love, I will not hold back a second time. Your raids will stop, or you all will die."

The prince nodded and stepped back, disappearing right before my eyes. I looked around, and it was only Ronin and me in the area next to the cave entrance. The ogres must have fled when the fighting commenced.

My heart swelled for the man who came to my rescue, even though I knew nothing would ever happen between us. I wished I could run to him and wrap my arms around him and cover him with kisses to show my love and gratitude.

He lowered his head and breathed in deeply. Then turning towards me, he made his way over and knelt before me.

"Where are you hurt?" His voice was shaking, and I put my hand on his arm to assure him I was okay.

"I'm fine Ronin, I just think it's bruised." I tried to move my leg to prove to him I was okay, but pain shot through it again and I gasped.

Suddenly, my face was pressed against his chest as he wrapped his arms around me.

"Lillian, I was such a fool." His voice choked with emotion. "How could I ever have let this happen to you." I wrapped my arms around him and pulled him closer, not caring that my leg was pulsing with pain.

"Let's help the poor girl first before you break her some more." I looked up to see who spoke and Caden was walking towards us, followed by his majesty. I quickly let go of Ronin and flushed at being caught embracing the commander.

"Here, I brought a tonic." His Majesty said as he reached into a leather pouch at his side and handed a small vial to me.

"Thank you, Your Majesty." I popped off the cork and drank its contents.

"It won't heal the injury to its fullest, but it should help with anything major."

A tingly feeling went down my leg soon after, and I moved my hip to see if it worked. I was grateful when the pain didn't shoot down my leg, but it was still uncomfortable.

"Thank you, Your Majesty. I can tell it is already working." I started to get up so we could head back to Llor and away from this awful place.

"Allow me, Lillian." Then Ronin swooped me up in his arms, and I threw my arms around his neck and gazed deeply into his eyes. It reminded me of the first time he rescued me all those months ago. First from my father, and now from ogres. I couldn't help but notice his gaze went to my lips. I looked around to see if his majesty and Caden were still here watching what was happening between us, not wanting to share this intimate moment with an audience.

"They left through the portal." He told me as if he had read my thoughts. Realizing we were alone now made my stomach drop and my heart race as I became even more aware of just how close I was to him. I couldn't help it as my gaze went back to his lips. Looking back up into his eyes I noticed they burned with longing, as I knew mine did. He slowly set me down on my feet, and I was grateful pain did not shoot through my leg. He kept one hand on my back while the other reached up to cup my face, then brushed back to my neck, his fingers entwining in my hair. My face filled with heat as his thumb ran up and down my neck, leaving a line of tingles wherever he touched. He leaned down slowly, and I pushed up on my toes to finally kiss the man I knew I had loved for a long time.

Chapter 23

RONIN

I didn't want the kiss to end. She was perfect, right here in my arms where she should have been from the very beginning. I wasted so much time trying to fight my feelings for her when I should have been loving her.

So, instead, I deepened our kiss and put both hands in her hair, bringing her closer to me. She grunted in pain, and I immediately released her.

"Are you okay?" I looked down at her leg.

"Yes, it's just sore and…"she paused and even though it was dark, the moonlight showed me her face was crimson with a blush.

"What is it?" I asked her while tenderly grabbing her chin and lifting it up to meet my gaze.

"It's only from being on my toes from our…" she smiled and bit her lip, looking away from me.

I bent down and swooped her up in my arms once more, and a giggle left her lips as she wrapped her arms around my neck. It was a glorious sound, and I vowed I would make her laugh for the rest of our days.

"Is that better?"

She nodded, and I knew I had to tell her what a fool I'd been.

"Lillian, I am sorry for how I treated you. You deserve someone so much better than me, but I have realized I can't live without you. Not now, not ever. I was blinded by pride, and I know that now. I am glad I lost that wager, and I'd do it all again if I could just have you as my bride." I paused knowing she had every right to reject me with how I had treated her. "If you'll have me?"

"Ronin, that is all I have ever wanted."

I bent down and captured her lips to mine once more, my heart soaring with her response. She tightened her hold on me and deepened our kiss. Not wanting it to end, I opened the portal and stepped through with her still in my arms, vowing never to let her go again.

THE END.

First, I want to thank my Heavenly Father who is always inspiring me in my books and the guidance he gives me.

Also, a huge thank you to my readers…it's because of you that I write these stories.

Follow me on Facebook, Instagram, TIKTOK, and Amazon for more updates and new releases!

Printed in Dunstable, United Kingdom